CW00621531

'A tale of a treasure hunt, with the Bible providing clues: a highly enjoyable read, and an edifying one. Strongly recommended.'
Professor Peter Scott, Director of the Lincoln Theological Institute based at Manchester University

'I became involved: led through a puzzle and along the way I am introduced to a spectrum of well-portrayed people, each different in personality and circumstance – a telling cross section of any parish. Incorporation of modern media, bloggers and search engines make it all very realistic. Many of the trite dictums of Church teaching are given a new relevance. Pass it on!'
Bud Young, magazine editor and landscape consultant

'With characters that pop, spirited dialogue and puzzles that pull you in, this book will keep you reading until the last surprising page.'
Wendy H Jones, author of the award-winning DI Shona McKenzie *mysteries*

The Kilfinan Treasure

Harry Hunter

instant
apostle

First published in Great Britain in 2019.

Instant Apostle
The Barn
1 Watford House Lane
Watford
Herts
WD17 1BJ

British Library Cataloguing-in-Publication Data

A catalogue record for this book is available from the British Library

This book and all other Instant Apostle books are available from Instant Apostle:

Website: www.instantapostle.com

E-mail: info@instantapostle.com

ISBN 978-1-912726-05-9

Printed in Great Britain.

Author's note

Information about the saints mentioned in this book has been drawn from multiple sources. However, reliable details about the 'Celtic' saints are sparse and sometimes fanciful, while sources may be inconsistent and contradictory. Although all the featured saints were real, my references to aspects of their lives and works should not be taken too literally.

Contents

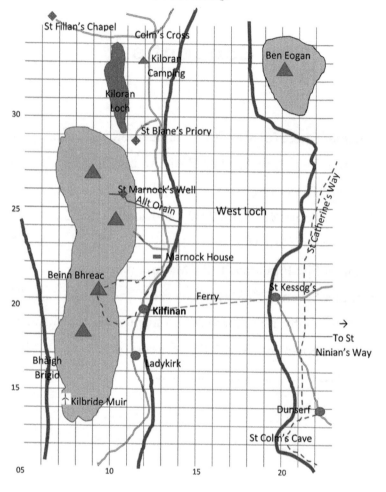

Kilfinan and its Surroundings

Chapter One

27th May 2017
Endgame

A satisfied smile suffused Tom Hodson's face. His eyes alighted on St Finnan's noticeboard, which welcomed him to the Scottish Episcopal Church. He took a moment to absorb its details before walking purposefully to the main door. He must have entered rather brusquely because a man in clerical garb turned his head with a start, before resuming his daily routine.

'Might I see the rector?' the visitor asked.

The cleric again lifted his head, this time paying more attention. Tom detected an expression of dawning realisation.

'You mean my wife, Penny. I'm just the lay reader. Can I help you?'

Tom wasn't familiar with the niceties of Episcopal officialdom. Indeed, the reply confirmed his preconceptions and prejudices about Byzantine Church hierarchies. But by now he harboured a grudging admiration for the clergy of St Finnan's; he remained gracious.

'Tom Hodson,' he said, holding his hand out towards the cleric.

'Sam Waite,' the lay reader reciprocated. 'Are you a visitor?'

'Just up from Cheshire for a couple of nights. I've never been north of the border before.' Tom steadied his nerves. 'Might I see inside the vestry?'

Sam seemed unable to suppress a nervous chuckle. Tom felt reassured and began to relax. The phlegmatic cleric, however, had suddenly become animated. 'Of course! Come this way,' he spluttered.

They walked towards the transept and Sam opened a door into a modest room, bathed in rays of late-afternoon sun. Tom was surprised at the tranquil beauty of the space. He looked at what he had come to see; it was even simpler to spot the answer than he had imagined.

'Then I suppose it must be Mungo?' he ventured. 'Can I claim my prize?'

'With the greatest pleasure. Very well done! Let's go over to the rectory. Penny will be delighted to meet you.'

Sam again led the way and the visitor noted that he left the church unlocked. 'What a pleasant surprise; there are some parts of the country where you can still trust people,' he mused, with a touch of envy.

They breezed into the adjacent rectory, a mellow Edwardian building set in a well-stocked garden. It exuded contentment.

'Penny!' called Sam. 'There's a gentleman who was very keen to see our vestry.'

A muffled whoop echoed from above them and an elegant woman, grey-haired but curiously youthful, galloped down the stairs.

She beamed as her eyes met the similarly grey, but tall and distinguished, visitor. 'You've solved …?'

Before she could finish the question both men were nodding their heads like excited schoolboys.

Penny introduced herself and invited the guest to take a seat.

'Well then, let's have a look,' Sam announced as he went to a cabinet in the lounge. From a drawer, he produced a small box which he proudly brought through for Tom to see. Three pairs of eyes shone at its restrained elegance.

'I'm very touched,' said Tom. 'It's quite beautiful. Small but perfectly formed.' There was an unaccustomed lump in his throat.

'We should toast your success. Do you care for wine?' Penny asked.

'Red, if you have it.'

Penny returned in a minute with three glasses which were clinked in celebration. The initial nervousness quickly dissipated as they relaxed together.

Penny's curiosity seemed greater than Sam's. 'Is there a Mrs Hodson, might I ask? I imagine it might be fitting for a woman.'

Tom smiled inscrutably and lifted the prize towards his chest. 'Actually, I think it would look rather fetching in a tiepin. But, since you ask, there is shortly to be a second Mrs Hodson. I'm a widower who has unexpectedly found love late in life. You're right. I think Ruth will claim first dibs.'

'And is she in Kilfinan with you now?' enquired Sam.

'Oh no. She doesn't even know I'm here. I'm just staying at a guest house for a couple of nights.'

'Then you must join us for dinner,' announced Penny, emphatically.

After his efforts over the past twenty-four hours, Tom had an appetite for both food and company.

'We'll be ready by seven,' Sam continued. 'You can make yourself at home in the rectory until then.'

Tom declined the offer of an armchair in favour of returning to the church. He was happy to pass time studying the architectural details and browsing the notices. It was a beautifully calming place, especially in the douce light of early summer. He valued the time to pause and reflect.

Tom had come to realise that the vigour of a church could be deduced from its display of posters and pamphlets. You could work out the history of the building from its design and fitments, but it was the ephemera on the tables and walls which betrayed the pulse of the congregation. St Finnan's acquitted itself well, in his eyes: the notices on the wall were about poverty and injustice, about practical action. There was information about shared activities and outings. There was plenty of news. He discerned a skew to the elderly, but not as much as in many churches; youth activities were certainly in evidence. There were pamphlets and magazines to take away and a well-tended bookstall.

'Good for you,' he thought, as he sat down in a pew. He couldn't pray, but he could contemplate.

Sam had wondered if this moment would ever occur. He had feared his whimsical little escapade would either go unnoticed or else prove too abstruse and insoluble. Or alternatively that some member of St Finnan's might have an unfair advantage and spot the solution immediately. Evidently he need not have worried; Penny's well-judged assurances to the contrary had, as usual, proved accurate.

Still, he was curious to know how difficult it had proved and how much interest it had generated. And whether it had reached beyond the limited confines of people who read the local church notices. Penny shared his impatience but refrained from taking the initiative. She knew it was only fair to let Sam broach the matter with their guest: it should be his moment of satisfaction.

Sam's long background in industry had left him with good social skills and a sensitivity to the protocols of table talk. His affable and sometimes bumbling demeanour cloaked a perceptive and diplomatic mind, especially when it came to raising matters of faith with non-church folk.

Dinner was not long underway when Sam risked turning the conversation to matters of religion. He was well experienced in judging the appropriate moment to do so, and adept in backing off at any hint of offence.

'Might I ask,' he ventured, 'whether you would consider yourself a person of faith?'

Tom shook his head. 'No, I'm a man of reason.'

The response didn't surprise Sam, who had instantly noted an air of the humanist about him.

'The two aren't incompatible,' Sam observed with an amiable smile.

'I was put off religion a long time ago. I find that the natural and social sciences offer me all the explanations I need.' And then, in a slightly mischievous tone, Tom added, 'I hope that doesn't mean you want the prize back?'

'No, you're OK,' Penny assured him. 'Some things are unconditional.'

Tom smiled. Apparently, he recognised the allusion. Sam was not surprised when Tom continued to express his views more openly.

'I was educated at a Jesuit school. You know, the full-on Catholic bit. For a while I was tempted by the priesthood. There were some wonderful teachers, people of great integrity. And there were a few ghastly ones. The recent revelations about abuse don't surprise me in the slightest. Overall, though, they were a good bunch who left me with a strong moral compass. And,' he added, almost as an afterthought, 'with a decent knowledge of the Bible. Which has just come in surprisingly handy!'

They laughed at the irony. Sam could tell from Penny's body language that curiosity was getting the better of her.

'How long had it been since you dipped into your Bible?' she enquired.

'Not as long as you might think,' Tom replied. 'Ruth, my fiancée, has a faith, which I find rather touching in a quaint sort of way. I sometimes have to check up on a verse so I can tease her accurately.'

'And now we've made you read it even more. How beastly!' Penny joshed. 'Be honest; how did you find it?'

'Well, I'll agree you picked the best bits,' Tom conceded. 'If the Church was all about forgiveness and love and neighbourliness, I'd have a good deal more time for it.

Jesus was basically a good guy. I just have difficulty in believing all the supernatural stuff.'

Sam and Penny exchanged a glance which said 'leave well alone', although Tom unexpectedly prolonged the discussion a little further.

'I'm intrigued about these Celtic saints that keep popping up around here. They're quite fashionable now, I understand. Ruth seems quite taken with them.'

Sam noted an expression of pleasant surprise in Penny, whose knowledge of the topic was quite extensive, borne of a genuine fascination.

'Well, to say that there's a single Celtic Christianity would be misleading,' she interjected. Sam held her gaze, concerned that she might go into lecture mode, but she added simply: 'There were many saints in this neck of the woods from the fourth century onwards and there are plenty of stories and legends associated with them. Some of the stories are pretty wacky but they contain a little truth and some good sentiments.'

Sam detected a wry smile on Tom's face, as if he was about to say the same about the Bible, so he added, pre-emptively: 'I think some of the interest is simply that people like the romance of the old. But that's no bad thing. Opening up the old paths can often be more rewarding than trying to invent new ones. The old saints seem to have emphasised simplicity and encounter. That often appeals to people these days; they feel that the Church is too bound up with hierarchy, administration and rules.'

'I'm not wedded to any particular tradition,' Penny admitted, 'but different traditions seem to meet different needs at different times. I think the less strident and patriarchal tone of the Celtic tradition may strike a chord with a younger generation.'

'I think you may be right,' Tom agreed. 'Can you tell me anything about St Finnan?'

'Not a lot,' Sam admitted. 'The historians can only glean bits here and there. We don't even know whether his name should be spelt with one N or two. It could even be an alternative for Winning.'

'Ah, yes. I saw a sign to Kilwinning on my way here. Possibly the same person?'

Sam raised his eyebrows. 'Maybe. Though we're pretty sure it relates to an Irish monk of the seventh century. He trained at Iona Abbey and then became Bishop of Lindisfarne.'

'So not much later than Aidan,' Tom observed.

Penny and Sam shared their surprise at Tom's knowledge. 'Yes indeed, directly after,' Penny replied.

'The knowledge is still there. It's surprising what sticks from your schooldays. And comes in handy in pub quizzes.' After a few moments' silence, Tom added: 'And I have admiration for those early saints too. I might not share their religious conviction but I do admire their courage, sailing across the oceans by the stars in primitive boats. And then facing up to the restive pagan natives.'

'I think you'd have liked Finnan,' Penny said. 'He built a cathedral on Lindisfarne, but it was a typically Irish one. Hewn oak and a thatched roof; nice and simple. Led a very virtuous and saintly life by all accounts, devoting himself to good works.'

'And he must have been a courageous chap as well as a compelling preacher,' Sam continued. 'Converted a couple of tribal kings before travelling along the west of Scotland establishing church cells. Far too risky for my liking.'

'Now that's the sort of Christianity I can relate to,' Tom conceded. 'However did the Church lose its way so badly?'

'Because we're pilgrims and pilgrims often lose the way,' Penny suggested. 'I hope we're getting back on track now. But you know what people are like. When we're faced with secularism and decline we feel a need to take control of the situation. We want to plan and organise, take things into our own hands. Many of the early saints relinquished control, took risks and believed that God would provide encounters and opportunities. Maybe we can rediscover that.'

Tom grinned sympathetically. Penny's comment had given him food for thought, which he seemed to spend some moments digesting.

'I think Ruth would be very interested to meet you,' he observed, and then added: 'She would find you a kindred spirit. The ministry would have appealed to her, but of course it's far too late now.'

'Oh, never say never!' Sam chuckled after a brief hiatus. 'We were both well into middle age before we took the plunge. I trained part-time to be a reader and then Penny got envious!'

'Oh, don't exaggerate!' exclaimed Penny. 'My calling was entirely independent.'

Tom seemed amused at the sharpness of the exchange.

Sam retreated. 'Ah, all right then. Quite separate. I was an old-school engineer and a very traditional Anglican. I gradually found myself taking an interest in the spiritual welfare of my colleagues and friends. Ordinary folk who rarely or never went to church. I think they saw me as a "steady Eddie" sort of figure – someone who could lull them into a sense of security on personal matters.'

'Now then, Sam Waite, don't be unfair on yourself,' Penny giggled. 'It was only occasionally they called you "Old Makeweight".'

'To my face, at least,' Sam muttered.

'So did I hear you say Anglican?' Tom interjected. 'That doesn't sound very Scottish.'

'No, indeed,' Sam replied, detecting a safe line of conversation. 'We spent most of our life in Lincolnshire, working in business.'

'Lincoln has the most wonderful cathedral,' Tom sighed. 'I once attended a carol service there. Yes, even non-believers can enjoy that, you know.'

'Ah. We loved the place,' Penny concurred. 'And then, just as he qualified as a reader, Sam got posted up here with his work.'

Sam was pleased to hear her express it in those terms. At the time, she had accused him of selfishly accepting a promotion to a place where she had no desire to live.

'We didn't know what to expect up here,' Sam continued. 'But we were surprised at the opportunities.'

Penny nodded. 'Surprised by God, you might say. I persevered with my business interests while Sam discovered all manner of unexpected ways to minister to people.'

'And after Penny had finally accepted she was being called to "full-time" ministry, I was offered early retirement. It's been quite a ride.'

Sam noticed an expression of scepticism in Tom's face at the suggestion of divine guidance. Anticipating the possibility of a lengthy digression, he deflected the conversation.

'Now, what I'm really interested to know is ... how did you find my little game? Was it fun? Was it too easy? Was there much interest? How did you even find out about it? I don't imagine they sell many copies of the *Kilfinan Gazette* in Cheshire.'

Penny couldn't resist interjecting: 'I'm sure we could have trawled the internet to see if the puzzle was being followed, but Sam's far too self-conscious to do that. He'd be very upset if there was no evidence of interest and equally embarrassed if there was.'

Tom chuckled, as if wondering where to start.

At length, he explained how one of his fiancée's church friends was an inveterate social media networker. One day she posted a link to a blog which was trending from someone called Kilfie. This Kilfie, whoever they were, had copied a poem along with a few comments of their own. 'As soon as I saw it,' he concluded, 'I realised the poem was an acrostic. Well, I like word puzzles and sneaked back on to the site surreptitiously after she had gone out for the day.'

'And then what?' Penny prompted.

'So, I decided to follow Kilfie's blog and watched it gradually burgeon. Evidently it was attracting a great deal of attention. There was some sort of treasure hunt underway. Frankly, I couldn't resist it. I even took out a subscription to the online *Kilfinan Gazette*.'

'Even though the poems were clearly religious?' asked Sam.

'Well, it was the kind of religion I can handle. Not preachy. Just reflecting on some universal themes. And obviously written by someone with an impish sense of humour.'

'So, did you get the impression that there was a lot of interest?' Penny enquired.

'Oodles. Masses. You can infer all sorts of things from social media and internet traffic. Even the fact that the *Gazette* was giving space to the acrostics on the home page of its website.'

'I wonder if it made anyone blow the dust off their Bibles,' Sam pondered, more in hope than expectation.

'Well, if I'm anything to go by, plenty,' admitted Tom. 'I don't see what else you could do. I'll tell you something – if you wanted to get people reading …' He paused and raised his eyebrows. Sam and Penny completed the sentence with knowing smiles.

It was a thoroughly amicable evening and they chatted on into the night about life in Kilfinan, the busyness of retirement and, inevitably, about Tom's forthcoming wedding plans. Naturally it was a civil ceremony but Tom didn't entirely baulk at Sam's mischievous suggestion of the possibility of a church blessing.

Tom headed back to his guest house, happy not to have spent the evening alone and, indeed, to have enjoyed good-natured company. His visit had been entirely satisfactory and he would sleep well before returning to Cheshire.

Sam stacked the dishes after the meal and reflected on the outcome of the past few weeks. There would need to be an announcement in the *Gazette*. Perhaps an article. Best not to let it go to his head. He felt that something bigger had been at work here than just some modest local talent. Something much bigger.

Chapter Two

12th April 2017
Humility

Helen Finlay rarely bought the *Kilfinan Gazette*. She failed to understand why a weekly newspaper could drum up so little news in such a lively little town. Such was her reputation as a fount of local knowledge she could have easily filled the *Gazette*'s pages several times over with far more interesting stories. But it was Easter week. She felt it important to purchase a copy to peruse the church notices and consult the services being offered by the town's various denominations.

Her Sunday attendance was no longer as assiduous as it had been prior to widowhood, something for which she made excuses without ever accepting her culpability in upsetting several former friends at Kilfinan's Church of Scotland. Her late husband regularly used to check her quick tongue before it resulted in discord but, unrestrained and without malice aforethought, she had managed to fall out with numerous acquaintances in the congregation.

Her last visit to the kirk had included a spat with Wendy McAlister about the lack of crockery for post-service refreshments. The use of recyclable cardboard cups, she snapped, might be convenient for the catering team but she deemed it common and inhospitable. Wendy had retorted with a comment about volunteers having better things to do than spend half an hour washing up after everyone else had gone home.

In truth, the spat had been nothing like as public and acrimonious as Helen had imagined, and few had given it a second thought or could now even recollect it. But in Helen's memory it remained vivid. It was the last in a series of unpleasantries which had led to her continued absence for several months.

Easter, though, was a different matter and she could not let it pass without attending a traditional service. Further, she would press her daughter Naomi to accompany her to whichever service she decided upon. She doubted if Naomi had set foot inside a church since moving in with her feckless partner, and it troubled her that their out-of-wedlock baby had never been baptised. But it was high time that Naomi was reminded that at Easter even she could be expected to occupy a pew.

Helen scanned the articles in the *Gazette*'s pages contemptuously. The only report which told her anything she did not know already was an update on the proposed new wind farm, including the date for a forthcoming public meeting. She muttered to herself about the proposal being a foregone conclusion and then muttered further about the dismal standard of reporting. She eventually found the information for which she had bought the paper squeezed in between the second-hand-car adverts and the football reports.

For such a modestly sized town, there were a surprising number of church notices. Clearly several of the congregations were making a special effort for Easter, with meditations, walks of witness and enterprising family events. But as for an Easter morning service, there was nothing that succeeded in tempting her away from the Church of Scotland and Reverend Gilmour's sound preaching. She had once considered moving to the Episcopal church but was none too keen after it appointed a female priest.

Alongside the church notices, at the bottom right, was the customary *Thought for the Week*, which she enjoyed, except on the occasions when it was too liberal and woolly. In her view, it almost justified purchasing the paper. She was particularly pleased to see that this week it was by none other than the Reverend Gilmour himself. Despite its restriction to six column inches, it was a remarkably concise and complete defence of the reality of the resurrection and the defeat of infernal principalities. She could almost hear him declaiming it from the pulpit, which redoubled her resolve to attend his forthcoming service.

Adjacent to this column was something most curious. As an irregular purchaser of the newspaper she could not be sure that it was unprecedented, but it was certainly highly unusual. She wasn't even sure that it should be among the church notices at all. A poem of sorts had been posted without any acknowledgement or title or explanation. It read:

Humility will be
Essential; prayers
Are what you'll need;
Like Solomon in his
Temple, asking heaven's
Hosts to intercede,
Entreating God to heal the
Land and heal the people's pain.
And hereby Treasure you may gain:
Note the verse, and you may succeed –
Do it in hope, not from greed.

It immediately rang a bell: the reference to Solomon gave it away. Surely it was an allusion to his dedication prayer after he had finished building the temple in Jerusalem? She felt smug at recognising the connection so quickly. But why had it been posted and by whom? And what was she meant to make of the last three lines?

Curiosity made her return to the poem that evening. She enjoyed puzzles. An avid reader of detective novels, she fancied her skills as an armchair sleuth.

The starting point must surely be to visit the relevant Bible passage. Confidently, she went to First Kings to locate Solomon's prayer. She experienced a pang of self-reproach: it must have been years since she had read that section of the Old Testament. While her husband was alive she had conscientiously observed a quiet time each morning, a discipline which had often helped her to maintain an equilibrium throughout the day. Her day would never feel right if it had not included an early-morning Bible reading.

She had never understood why some folk found the Old Testament dull: to Helen, its great sweep of historical events and people had always been vivid and captivating. She recalled the first time she read the account of Solomon's temple: how she had been enthralled and swept up in its romance and scale and beauty and majesty. She could visualise all the wonderful craftsmanship. She could almost see Solomon bedecked in his finery and hear the thunderous phalanx of skilled musicians. It was a passage she had once known well.

But despite a careful search, the desired verse eluded her. After fruitlessly wading through a mass of details about construction and decorative artwork it began to dawn on her that she was looking in the wrong place. Of course, the account of the temple and Solomon's prayer was repeated in Chronicles. Helen reproached herself. Half an hour later, after starting at chapter 1 of First Chronicles and ploughing through interminable historical and genealogical records, she eventually located what she was looking for. It must have been the longest chunk of the Old Testament she had ever read in one sitting, but there in the seventh chapter of the Second Book of Chronicles she found what she was after – the memorable reply when God responds to Solomon's dedication prayer:

> If my people, who are called by my name, will humble themselves and pray and seek my face and turn from their wicked ways, then I will hear from heaven, and I will forgive their sin and will heal their land.

She was certain that this was what the newspaper entry had referred to. But why had the poet not simply quoted Second Chronicles 7:14? And what on earth was she to make of the last three lines of the poem which seemed to have little connection to the verse? They seemed to allude to some sort of treasure. Perhaps it was allegorical. Easter was, after all, the time to remember the greatest Treasure of all, as well as a time when children went on treasure hunts for hidden eggs. These days, more of them seemed to believe in the Easter bunny than Jesus.

'At least,' she pondered, 'it will get people thinking. It would be no bad thing if people hereabouts did show a bit more humility and listen to the voice of God.' Helen often harboured such opinions.

Easter Sunday started with azure skies and a sharp, low-angle sunshine backlighting the eastern hills. Helen checked herself in the mirror before setting off for church in good time, as she expected the car park to fill up quickly. It was too bad that Naomi had dreamed up a feeble excuse not to attend: Helen was perhaps less concerned about her daughter's spiritual welfare than about not getting a lift, even though she was perfectly capable of driving herself. She spent the journey harbouring uncharitable thoughts towards Naomi, and it was an effort to nod politely at the lady on door duty as she received a copy of the week's notices.

The church was half full and, while affording Helen an opportunity to judge silently people who didn't bother to attend on this most important day of the year, this also allowed her to select an anonymous seat. She scanned those present with impassive interest, noting the sprinkling she might still count as friends. She nodded a polite greeting to a pair of unknown worshippers who arrived alongside her.

As the Reverend Archie Gilmour rose to his feet she noticed how elderly he looked. The wiry, indefatigable hillwalker now appeared aquiline and grey. But when the time came for the sermon, his voice was as strong as ever and age seemed to have bestowed an even more impassioned reverence.

It was Easter. He spoke of sacrifice. He spoke of suffering as well as resurrection. Helen knew it would not be a service for faint-hearts who wanted easy answers and fuzzy imagery. Archie was uncompromising. Perhaps it was as well that Naomi wasn't there.

But then he changed tack. Instead of continuing his exposition about the empty tomb, he suddenly challenged his congregation to examine themselves. 'What do you need to sacrifice?' he thundered at them, shaking a bony fist. 'What would be the costliest thing that you could surrender today? Might it be your pride?'

Then to her surprise, he paraphrased the passage in Second Chronicles: 'If you will humble yourselves and pray and seek God's face and turn from your wicked ways, *then* God will hear from heaven and will forgive your sin. Even the great King Solomon was willing to do that. Are you? Permit me an anecdote …'

Helen knew this signalled an allusion to the mountains.

'I've learned to treat the hills with humility. Even when starting to tackle a rock face I've climbed a score of times I have to consciously banish my pride and self-confidence. The deceptive beauty of the Highlands always needs to be treated with respect.' And so he went on to expound how an overhang in the Arrochar Alps had once humbled him and left him fearing for his life.

Helen wondered if it was Archie who had written the poem. But perhaps not. The tenor of his voice didn't sound like someone playing games.

'Isn't it sad,' he continued in his measured but penetrating voice, 'that some of us still harbour grudges and feuds with each other? Even some in this congregation will not sit next to each other. Some people in front of me now are hardly on speaking terms with members of their own family. I challenge you this Easter to humble yourselves. To search yourselves for any root of bitterness and lay it at the cross.'

Was he looking at Helen? How could he have been? He must have prepared his sermon days before and could not have known she would attend. The knowledge that she was just one sinner among many did not make her feel any more comfortable.

If the Reverend Gilmour had directed any of his words specifically at Helen, it did not show after the service as he greeted the faithful in the refreshments room.

'Happy Easter, Mrs Finlay. How delightful to see you. I'd missed you lately. I do hope you've been well.'

She nodded, before venturing: 'I was delighted to see your column in the *Gazette*, Archie. Very telling. And, by the way, did you write the poem beside it?'

The Reverend Gilmour raised his eyebrows. 'No. Nothing to do with me. I haven't a clue. Perhaps whoever it was will reveal themselves next week.' Then he added,

'Mrs McAlister was mentioning you to me. There she is by the bookstall. Why don't you go and join her?'

Helen could hardly refuse, for she could see the growing queue waiting for their moment with the minister.

Wendy McAlister's face lit up as she saw Helen, and it was clear that she had let bygones be bygones. Her comments were entirely gracious and complimentary. She was a cheerful and good-natured soul and, after chatting for ten minutes over coffee, they agreed to meet on Tuesday at the Harbour Lights café.

On returning home, Helen checked over the entry in the paper again in case there were any hidden clues that she hadn't spotted first time around, but to no avail. Her confidence in her sleuthing skills was dented. She sat down and returned to the relevant passage in Second Chronicles. The more closely she read it the more deeply she was struck by the sheer humility of Solomon, at least at that stage of his life. Here he was, the most splendidly rich and wise man in the world, who surrendered himself completely to God.

She turned a forensic eye to the account in case it contained pertinent hints. She noted in chapter 6 how Solomon had 'stood on the platform and then knelt down before the whole assembly of Israel and spread out his hands towards heaven'. She pondered his wisdom in realising that even the most fabulous temple could not contain God. She reflected that all this was done to create a space where God might give attention to the people's prayers. Solomon must have realised that, kingly though he was, he was no more than a humble servant in the eyes of God.

It was as if the poem and the Bible passage spoke to her directly, in the same way as Archie's sermon. It was a passage she thought she knew well and yet which she now read as if for the first time. It was personal.

'If my people, who are called by my name, will humble themselves and pray and seek my face ...' the passage had said. 'Humility will be Essential ...' the poem had begun. And that prayer would be needed. Helen thought about her forthcoming meeting with Wendy. She wondered about extending an olive branch to Naomi, something which would not come easily. With the words almost choking in her throat she forced herself to pray about the situation. She even promised God she would try to be less vain. Her words felt rather vapid and contrived, but at least it was a start.

Tuesday morning saw her at the Harbour Lights with Wendy, having made an effort to look her best and actually appear as if she was looking forward to renewing their acquaintance. They were blessed with another of Kilfinan's cloudless spring skies and a bustle of activity across the sea loch. Helen talked about her holidays and the books she was reading, hoping to deflect Wendy from more contentious and painful topics. She was still resentful of certain things that had been said between them, and deeply sensitive to the possibility that various wagging tongues at the church remained judgemental about her daughter's unwedded relationship with an unsuitable man. The topic was one which she preferred to withhold from the public domain, and she trusted that people now regarded it as being off-limits.

But Helen had not bargained for Wendy's memory, razor-sharp for a seventy-eight-year-old. 'And how is Naomi doing, and that charming young man of hers? Kenneth, isn't it?'

It was too sudden a question for Helen, who responded with an ill-considered comment about her disappointment with Naomi. It was not the conversation she was hoping for; nor was it the answer she would have given if she had applied a little more forethought. Wendy must have noticed her bristle but continued nonetheless.

'Don't judge her too harshly, dear,' Wendy responded in tones as sanguine as Solomon's. 'Young people are under a lot of pressure these days. She probably needs encouragement rather than criticism. And don't, whatever you do, lose contact with your new grandson. Naomi and Kenneth are ambitious and could leave the village for pastures new at any time. Don't waste precious moments lecturing them about morality, however much you might care for your daughter's soul.'

Helen nodded. It was the start of a long and entertaining discussion which ended with them agreeing to make Tuesday mornings a regular fixture.

And that evening Helen phoned her daughter with an offer of a coffee-and-walnut cake and some babysitting.

Chapter Three

19th April 2017
Wistful

Naomi Finlay had just settled baby David and was apprehensively awaiting the arrival of her mother. The offer of a cake and babysitting seemed too good to be true and she was certain there had to be an ulterior motive, which probably had something to do with judgement and salvation.

Helen arrived, however, with disarming candour and, after an affectionate hug, breezed through to the kitchen to fill the kettle. As it came to the boil, she produced a freshly baked cake. She sliced two generous portions and brought them to the table without a hint of an agenda.

As she laid them down she noticed a copy of the latest edition of the *Kilfinan Gazette* on the table.

'I didn't think you bought the local rag, dear. You always used to joke about how pathetic it was.'

'Oh, I think everybody's bought it this week.'

Naomi often said surprising things, occasionally ones intended to shock, but this reaction was bizarre in its ordinariness. The newspaper's circulation was modest, its readership fickle and predominantly elderly. Why should a young mum make a sweeping statement about everyone buying it?

Naomi apparently noted her mother's quizzical look. 'I thought you might have read the religious page,' she continued enigmatically.

'Well, I did last week. To check the church services which you didn't want to come to.' Helen bit her tongue. 'But we won't go into that.'

'Didn't you notice anything, well... unusual?'

Helen reflected for a moment or two. She moderated her voice: 'You aren't referring to that curious poem next to Archie Gilmour's column, are you?'

'Of course I am,' Naomi laughed. Helen's bemusement intensified, and she noticed a dawning realisation in her daughter's face. 'But then, you don't while away your idle moments browsing the internet, do you?'

Helen checked herself. She was barely through the door and already at risk of launching into a religious monologue, something which could easily snowball into a row. She sat down, thinking how to pursue a spiritual direction without hectoring. Naomi sat beside her.

'Well,' Helen recommenced, 'I read the poem, but it seemed very religious. I can't imagine it caused much excitement.'

'Oh, believe me, it's causing quite a stir.'

'Well, I can't understand why. It struck me as well-intentioned but a little clumsy. What's so special about it?'

'You mean apart from the obvious?'

Helen was uncharacteristically silent, awaiting an explanation. Naomi would hardly have used the word 'obvious' about a verse from Second Chronicles.

'I mean,' continued her daughter, 'it was an acrostic.'

Helen felt her expression turn blank.

'The first letter of each line spelt out "Heal the Land". Beyond that I didn't know what to make of it, though it reminded me of something vaguely familiar.'

Helen felt surprised and a little saddened. Surprised because a lover of detective fiction like herself should have noticed such a patent clue. How could she have missed it? And saddened because at one time Naomi would have instantly twigged the allusion to Solomon in his temple. She had been such a star at Sunday school and had remained loyal to church right through her teens. Now, as with so many of her peers, she had forsaken her first love and retained only a nominal association.

In her younger days Naomi had taken seriously the warning in 2 Corinthians 6 about not being unevenly yoked with a non-believer. She had become engaged to a boy who occasionally attended youth fellowship and Helen had made elaborate mental plans for a traditional wedding. But life had presented messier choices. Naomi realised she had made the commitment too young and extricated herself, strongly against her parents' wishes, from what she knew would be an unhappy match. Kenneth, a trainee mechanic, had caught her on the rebound and had been a tower of strength to her after the sudden death of her father.

A year later they moved into a flat and wagging tongues succeeded in driving her away from church altogether. She had hoped her mother would have accepted her choice but instead was met with incessant accusations about how a widow's grief was being compounded by a daughter's sin. In truth, no matter how much time Naomi had let elapse after her father's death, she would have met with the same accusations. Anyway, she had a life to get on with and there were friends who would accept her even if others didn't.

Helen found herself ruminating about her daughter's lifestyle and loss of Bible knowledge. But her recent encounter with Wendy had taught her a lesson in tolerance. She told her mind to stop wandering and to concentrate on the relatively simple task of enjoying a tea and chat with her daughter while glancing admiringly at her snoozing grandson.

She settled her distracted thoughts. 'Silly me,' she said. 'Heal the Land. I should have spotted that. Anyway, it hadn't occurred to me to buy the *Gazette* this week. What's so special that everyone wants a copy?'

'Another acrostic, look.'

Naomi turned to the church notices and pointed out the anonymous poem in the column alongside the *Thought for the Week*.

> Creativity, wisdom, compassion,
> Love and clay – these are required
> As the basic ingredients to fashion
> You and me – when the mixture is fired
> At the kiln of God's pottery.
> Now, think on this as you seek Treasure:
> Do not think life's gain is mere lottery.
> Pressed down, running over is God's measure,

Offering wealth of a different kind –
Take time to ponder and recollect
That you are lovingly wrought and uniquely
    designed.
Even wild flowers are beautifully bedecked;
Rough materials may be wondrously refined.

Helen read it aloud as Naomi followed.

'Clay and Potter,' said the daughter, noting the initial letters. 'I remember something about God being the potter and us being the clay. Do you think that's what it's about?'

Helen knew instantly that it referred to Isaiah 64 and was on the point of directing her daughter to the relevant passage. But she decided it would be better to let Naomi research it for herself. It would do her good to refresh her knowledge of God's Word rather than having the answer spoon-fed. She simply nodded and, with a glint in her eye, asked: 'Who do you think can be doing it and why?'

'Well, according to the local grapevine, there may be some sort of treasure hunt. Someone's even started a blog on it. I think that's why *The Gazette* is selling out. It certainly can't be because of the news content. Look, there's a reference to a treasure again. It's got a capital T, same as last week.'

'Oh dear, the morals of this world. Everyone wants something for nothing. I'm sure it just refers to the treasure of God's blessing.'

Naomi didn't disabuse her. She nodded assent, while adding, 'But why does it have a capital T? Don't you think there might be an actual treasure?'

It was a good point, and one which stoked up Helen's interest in reapplying her sleuthing skills. She tried not to betray her rare sensation of excitement. Anyway, if she pursued the matter it would turn into a Bible study, and that wasn't what she had come for. It was time to change the topic.

'Now, when would you like me to babysit for David?'

'When can you manage?'

'Well, to be honest, I haven't exactly got a crowded diary.'

'We'd love to get to the MiniCine tomorrow night, if that's OK.'

It was many decades since Kilfinan had had a picture house and the periodic visits of the mobile cinema were a boon. The film currently showing had received some criticism in the pages of the *Gazette* for its amorality and Helen almost protested. But she knew what it was like to try to get 'me-time' away from a baby and decided this was more important than suggesting her daughter go to something more edifying. She agreed, and witnessed Naomi's eyebrows raise in surprise.

After Helen had gone, the baby was still sleeping soundly. Naomi knew there were a score of urgent things she should be doing during this fleeting respite but the lure of the acrostic was too strong. She would never have asked her mother for help, which would have invited a sermon. And she was sheepish about not being able to navigate the Old Testament: at one time it would have been second nature.

She remembered something about a prophet talking about clay. She Googled 'you potter we clay' and instantly received a result which, curiously, appeared to be climbing its way up the search algorithm. There, within a matter of seconds, was Isaiah 64:8:

> Yet you, LORD, are our Father.
> We are the clay, you are the potter;
> we are all the work of your hand.

It sounded familiar yet distant, hinting wistfully at happier days in the past when life had seemed more straightforward and carefree.

Naomi experienced a strong and unexpected wave of nostalgia. Her eyes moistened as, without warning, she recalled life as a teenager in the youth fellowship, full of so much friendship and sharing. And there was something else. She acknowledged that, deep down, she harboured a sadness at what she had lost by letting go of church connections. She had left because of hypocrisy and criticism. But she had also cast aside the acceptance and camaraderie she had once known among Christian friends.

The passage in Isaiah reminded her of the faith she had once enjoyed, full of powerful ideas of love and belonging. Now it had given way to the busyness of work and motherhood, the complications of a relationship and domestic finances, and the judgemental words of her mother and former church acquaintances. She wondered if it was lost forever or whether it might be possible sometime to make a fresh start.

She was lapsing into daydreams, which annoyed her. Drifting thoughts were a lost opportunity. Nowadays, she could ill afford to waste precious moments.

Naomi retrieved her Bible which, out of embarrassment, she had tucked away from Kenneth's gaze. He was not sympathetic to the Church and Naomi was happy to leave such matters on the back burner. Her partner came from a Roman Catholic family but neither he nor his siblings now attended Mass. Naomi figured this was because most of his peers didn't 'do religion', or at least didn't admit to it publicly. Besides, he had grown up on Clydeside and had more than once expressed relief at being away from the sectarianism experienced in his youth.

Even in a friendly backwater like Kilfinan, the fact that he had been to St Munnu's School had blighted more than one job interview. Naomi couldn't comprehend why going to a school named after a battle soldier of the Celtic saints could be thought of as a bad thing. But Kenneth assured her it had been bad enough to have stones and insults hurled at him by big children from the other school.

Naomi knew that Kenneth, despite his apparent lack of faith, secretly admired the 'hard man' abbot preaching firmness of faith long before the Church split itself into warring factions. Long-standing legend held that Munnu had spent his final days near Kilfinan; more recently, archaeologists had located relics which gave credence to this story. When this had been reported on the local news, Kenneth had commented that Munnu was 'his kind of Christian'. One that reminded him of the best of his teachers, the ones with a quiet faith and sense of decency. With good reason, though, he sometimes spoke less fondly of other teachers, memories of whom continued to cast a pall over his view of the Church.

Naomi could hear the baby starting to wake. Quickly, she returned to the two acrostics to see if they gave any further clue about a mysterious 'Treasure'. She had to resort to the chapter list in her Bible to locate books that once she would have found as easily as recipes in her go-to cookbook.

Apart from the fact that the acrostics both related to the Old Testament there seemed to be no apparent link. She looked at Second Chronicles, speed-reading several chapters in the hope that seeing the bigger picture would shed light on the specific verse. Her mind boggled at the sheer scale of events as she read the passage. The number of animals sacrificed seemed both repugnant and fascinating at the same time. She recalled what she had once been taught about the perfect sacrifice putting an end to old rituals. The knowledge was still there. Nostalgia momentarily returned.

The account of Solomon's temple had been vaguely familiar but as she scanned it yet again it suddenly started to come alive; Second Chronicles, which had once seemed so turgid, was now rich with circumstance and characters. Then she stumbled on a verse in chapter 6 long forgotten but which had once struck her as a great truth:

> But will God really dwell on earth with humans? The heavens, even the highest heavens, cannot contain you. How much less this temple that I have built!

She remembered a moment in her teens when she had suddenly grasped the powerful idea that God wasn't confined to particular buildings. At the time, the revelation had seemed almost subversive. She had become progressively disillusioned with the church of her parents and its constant obsession with raising money to maintain crumbling buildings. 'All that,' she had thought, 'for a God that doesn't even dwell in buildings. I could just as well be worshipping God at home or in the park, with no minister ranting on about what a sinner I am.'

Looking, now, at the passage with more mature eyes, she wondered if she had been entirely fair. Even though Solomon's ceremony was so peculiar and ancient, she started to understand why particular buildings might help her to encounter God and share fellowship with other believers. After all, she knew in her heart that it was people who made a church. A few of them she still counted as friends. Even some of the older people had radiated wisdom and kindness, managing to rise above what she had perceived as general hypocrisy and narrow-mindedness.

David began to gurn more insistently. Time was pressing. She turned to Isaiah, scanning the pages around 64:8. It didn't make easy reading. This was the vengeful God: the 'Mr Angry' which she had increasingly seen in her fellow churchgoers. Yet at the same time it contained some beautiful turns of phrase. Amid all the problems of his day, Isaiah had never lost sight of God's caring nature. Naomi dwelt on her memories of a creative, caring God, something which she had never fully lost.

But for all the potential relevance of the passage, it was in reality about Jerusalem in the very distant past. She could see no way of relating it to Kilfinan in the present day. 'Is someone trying to warn us that the world is being laid waste? That we need to repent? Is that why they have posted the acrostics?' After a few moments' consideration she decided against this explanation. The author did not come across as a doomsayer. The poems had a playful feel to them, and the selected verses were loving and kind. And anyway, why would they have chosen the *Kilfinan Gazette* as their mouthpiece?

Whatever, it was time to get on with the day. She couldn't daydream. David was now well awake and needing attention. Kenneth would soon be back from work, needing a good meal. She was itching to tell him about going to MiniCine. She tried to set aside thoughts about the Old Testament God of winepresses, blood-spattered garments and vengeful swords. They reminded her too much of a church that stood for rules and regulations, sanctimonious proverbs and declamatory preachers.

Still, as she played with David she remembered Isaiah's images of a new heaven and a new earth. She recalled one distant but inspirational sermon about judgement and mercy being two sides of the same coin. It was one of those rare occasions, she had felt at the time, when the minister was really communicating with people's hearts and minds.

Perhaps she had misunderstood the idea of judgement and had let this drive her away from church. Since an early age she had been attracted to a church which sought justice rather than neatly pressed tablecloths; she began to wonder whether she might not give it a second chance.

But none of this got her any closer to solving the puzzle and she resolved to reread the passages for the rest of the week. And she would read around them and meditate on their meaning. Just in case something dawned on her about the Treasure.

Chapter Four

26th April 2017
Burden

Graham Coe stared with trepidation at the front page of the *Gazette*. 'Sparks Fly at Wind Farm Meeting', the headline read. He carried it across to the counter.

'Selling like hot cakes again,' the assistant said with a knowing grin.

Graham was not in on the secret. Innocently, he replied, 'It's this wind farm business. They always cause a fuss.'

The assistant wrinkled her brow.

As Graham waited for his change he skimmed the article. His own name was there several times, but he had been treated benignly. He was relieved not to be cast as the town's villain.

Graham did not particularly enjoy staying in Kilfinan, only seeing his family at weekends. The *Anam Cara* guest house was perfectly clean and comfortable and Katie Smith was a polite and obliging proprietress, but it was hardly the high life. Still, he had to do the bidding of his employer which was now branching out from fossil fuels to cleaner forms of energy, frequently involving wind farms in Scotland. As ever, the Kilbride Muir proposal was dividing the community, even though it already supported a small cluster of generators. Public acceptance of wind farms was slowly increasing, but unfortunately so was their scale, which in turn fuelled new opposition. It was his job to present the schemes to the local public and seek to win the necessary consents, something which could be a thankless task. He often regretted leaving his back-room job in electrical engineering, safe from the public gaze.

Most people, he suspected, were neutral towards the schemes, but there were always well-organised pressure groups shouting him down with what he regarded as unscientific evidence. At times he wanted to tell them to shut up and let other people have a say. But he knew that his job was to keep calm, deflect the flak and not let his public relations façade slip. His company tried to be a good neighbour, operating well-managed sites which made fair contributions to community funds.

He headed to the Harbour Lights café where Rita stood cheerfully at the counter. It was just after half past five, nearly time for her to start cleaning the tables and shut up shop. He knew she would have been run off her feet since early-bird breakfasts. Graham had been her habitual last customer ever since he arrived in Kilfinan, but she never showed a flicker of irritation. Indeed, her face lit up, as if she knew he was in urgent need of a smile and a friendly word. Even at the day's end she never appeared exhausted. If Graham ever felt any sense of self-pity, Rita made him feel guilty, in an appreciative sort of way.

Her greeting of 'The usual, Mr C?' received a jaded nod on his part.

A baked potato, portion of coronation chicken and the remnants of the day's salad had been kept in reserve; one day he might want something different. but for the moment he was content to be predictable and not to spring any unexpected surprises so close to six o'clock. There were precious few eateries in Kilfinan and Rita was an indispensable lifeline.

'I see you've bought the *Gazette*, Mr C. Are you joining in the treasure hunt?'

'You've got me there,' he replied.

Several ears pricked up at other tables.

'Come on, Graham, everyone's talking about it,' she retorted. 'Someone's posting strange little poems in the church notices section of the *Kilfinan Gazette*. It's not often you get people talking about something religious.'

Graham was none the wiser. 'So, what does this treasure hunt involve?' he asked, trying to put himself on the front foot, as if he were fielding questions from an audience.

'You've got to solve riddles in poems where each line starts with a significant letter. It's a bit too clever for me. People seem to think there's a treasure hunt because each time treasure's mentioned it's spelt with a capital T. Don't tell me you haven't noticed?'

Graham shrugged and sat, as was his custom, at an inconspicuous corner table. He flicked through the main contents of the paper before turning to the church notices. He had never previously consulted them – not out of antipathy, but because he never remained for the weekend. In fact, a large portion of joy had departed from his life in recent years and he had spasmodically wondered whether there might be a spiritual remedy.

As Rita predicted, there, by the weekly 'Godslot', he found a curious poem:

> When the world has made you weary,
> Empty, brittle, spent and teary
> And your life's full of irritations,
> Rife with rules and regulations,
> Your soul's in need of Gilead's balm,
> Freshets, oases, peace and calm:
> Invite the Lamb to join you there.
> No heavy yoke will He make you bear
> Dogma and doctrine He'll not demand,
> Rest sweetly in the palm of His hand
> Easily, lightly He'll help you recover,
> Servant King, outcast's lover –
> Treasure unfading He'll help you discover.

Graham looked at the initial letters – Weary Find Rest. He smiled ironically. The poem might have been written for him. He inhabited a world full of regulations – health and safety, planning, energy, legal, traffic. It was not what he had anticipated when he joined the company, but he was one of their few engineers who had turned out to have an aptitude for red tape and public relations, and it had afforded a promotion he couldn't refuse.

The poem was curious and cryptic, but to a lapsed Anglican like Graham it wasn't difficult to spot the allusion to a yoke that was easy to bear. Something about 'Come to me, all you who are weary and burdened'. He smiled at the irony – here he was, away from home, frazzled, harangued at meetings and with a phone that never stopped ringing. He heard the microwave ping. Sadly, it was a sound that stirred his spirit more than Beethoven's *Ode to Joy*. Rita's baked potatoes could surely match the finest in the world, all the better for having mellowed in the heated display unit for longer than was strictly wise.

Rita brought his rations over along with a mug of strong tea which he had forgotten to request. She craned her neck to see what he was perusing. 'Good luck with the poem,' she smiled. 'It's got me stumped.'

Heads nodded in agreement at other tables.

'Oh, and something else that may help you,' she added. 'Someone's started a blog. They're calling themselves Kilfie – not very imaginative, eh? Anyway, there are some interesting posts that might get you started.'

Graham wondered how she even found time to read the paper, but he supposed there would be lulls in the day when pondering a puzzle might provide a welcome distraction.

He read the poem several times over as he enjoyed his plateful. By the time he finished the café was, as ever, empty apart from himself and Rita. It was time to let her tidy the tables and shut up shop. He wondered what she went home to. Was it a hungry family demanding their evening meal? Did she live alone? Whatever her situation might be, she never complained.

Back in his room at *Anam Cara* he took the Gideons' Bible from the bedside table, something which he had done more than once during the long nights away from home. Usually it was out of boredom, but this time it was with a sense of purpose. Fortunately it had a foreword containing selections of helpful verses and there he quickly discovered that the piece about weary people finding rest related to Matthew 11:28. Graham checked it out. There at the end of the chapter were three verses about taking away heavy burdens. He sighed deeply.

'Why would someone write a cryptic poem about them, though?' he wondered. There was something a couple of verses earlier about things being 'hidden … from the wise and learned'. Things that might be 'revealed … to little children'. Was he trying too hard, applying an engineer's solution to something hiding in plain sight that was obvious even to a child? Was there a hint here about hidden treasure? Or was it just someone playing a game? Perhaps it was an inventive way of getting people to think about the Bible; something that would work better than preaching? If it was such a subterfuge, he didn't object to the author's gentle trickery.

He switched on his laptop and browsed the *Gazette*'s website in the hope that it might have copies of the preceding weeks' acrostics. He was rewarded with a summary of the poems to date and a commentary on their surprising popularity. Clearly, he was far from alone in his curiosity. And he had the advantage of time on his hands. Suddenly the long, homesick evenings had an upside. He used the search engine to locate chapter and verse for the other acrostics.

Graham read around the relevant chapters so extensively that he almost forgot to phone home. His wife sounded fractious at the lateness of his call. She'd been waiting to unload and launched into a verbal avalanche. He listened patiently to her tales of confrontation with their moody teenage daughter and couch-potato son. He heard the latest instalment of the office vendetta with her job-share partner. As the diatribe subsided, he gave her a potted account of his brushes with the Kilfinan public and sent her a photo of the *Gazette*'s front page, on which he was extensively quoted. He promised to get away early on Friday and reassured her that it wouldn't be much longer before he was returning to his usual office. Or at least until he was posted away to work on another new scheme, she reminded him. Of course, he'd remember to phone earlier tomorrow night.

They hung up and Graham texted the children with affectionately worded salvos to be a bit more helpful.

He lay down, staring at the ceiling. It was just after nine; the sky was still light and the street noisy. He hated being the absentee father and husband. One thought gyrated in his mind. 'Come to me, all you who are weary and burdened …' The other phrases had struck him equally. 'Pray and seek my face …' 'We are the clay, you are the potter …' He found the words attractive and wondered what it would be like actually to have a faith.

It took him a while to remember he was meant to be hunting for a 'Treasure'. The idea was silly, childish. He had far more important business to deal with. But it was a harmless distraction which, right now, suited him well.

He had considered the possibility that the poems might be just an allegory and that the hunt for an actual, material treasure might be vainglorious. But he clung to the possibility of a tangible prize. Something he could take back home to show the family. Graham was a natural problem-solver. He couldn't resist the challenge of a puzzle, especially one leading to a reward. But there was also a deeper if poorly articulated desire to bring some unexpected delight to his long-suffering family.

He looked again at the poems and passages to see if he could detect any pattern. He fancied he saw something in the repetition of certain words, in recurrent ideas, maybe even a numerical code in the verse numbers, but there was nothing strong enough to convince him he was on the cusp of a breakthrough.

He recalled what Rita had said about Kilfie the blogger and, after a quick internet search, located the site. It was rather clunky, he thought, as if the author was not very IT-savvy. Nor did it contain any clues about the blogger's identity, though from the commentaries on various posts Graham surmised that it was a person of faith. Rita had been right: the poems were certainly generating interest, although none of the posts told him anything he had not already guessed. If anything, they merely reinforced his view that the 'Treasure' might equally be metaphorical or real.

When darkness eventually came he quickly fell asleep, something which he hadn't anticipated. Billeted out in a provincial bed and breakfast, with his mind full of worries and work pressures, he was prone to insomnia. The following morning he experienced the rare luxury of being awoken by an alarm. He felt uncommonly refreshed. He even vaguely recalled his last dream of gliding weightlessly along a country lane, no briefcase or formal clothes to weigh him down. He was sorry to leave it in the realms of slumber as he pivoted mechanically out of bed.

Katie's fried tomatoes, bacon and egg promised to be even more reinvigorating than usual.

Arrival at his office brought a stark return to reality. There were slippages in schedules which had to be made up and multiple objections from consultees to be resolved. The company tried to be a good neighbour, but budgets were increasingly tight and negotiations with planners, residents' groups and the community council would need to be hard-nosed. Graham came away with more than his fair share of issues to sort out; the prospect of an early Friday departure began to recede ominously. He worked through his lunch and coffee breaks to make sure that Rita's baked potato didn't go to waste.

At 5.40 he entered the café with a bulging briefcase.

'Hello, Mr C,' Rita chirruped and he smiled in return. He was about to ask her how her day had been but was pre-empted.

'Any joy with those poems, Mr C?'

'No, not really. They're clever. Someone's playing a crafty little game with us. Maybe when I'm back home at the weekend I'll crack the code. Perhaps a change of environment will give me some inspiration.'

'I bet you did some unaccustomed reading, didn't you?' she whispered. Graham nodded. 'We're all doing it,' she winked.

Graham collected his tray, almost colliding with a young mother towing two fractious children as she went to settle her bill. He placed himself at the corner table and perused the uppermost of his briefcase's contents while mindlessly scooping the potato's filling into his mouth. It was nearly six o'clock when he finished; he was so engrossed in the planning committee's report on the wind farm that he hadn't noticed customers vacating the café.

He tidied his crockery and cutlery and returned the tray to the counter.

'Enjoy the rest of your evening, Rita,' he called.

She came through from the kitchen. 'Thank you, Mr C. You look like you'll be working late this evening.'

'May as well,' he replied. 'I'm not one for sampling Kilfinan's bohemian nightlife. Even if Thursday night is karaoke night at the King's Arms. What will you be up to?'

'Oh, I've got Mum to look after. She'll be needing to be fed and bathed.'

'Still got your Mum living at home?'

'Well, she's getting frail and we can't afford care-home fees. Anyway, it's company for me. You get into a routine.'

'Just the two of you?'

'Oh no, but my husband works late shifts at the warehouse. You know, the big shed at the top of town.'

'Doesn't sound like much of a rest.'

Rita smiled. 'I'm not one for resting. It's being busy that keeps me smiling.'

'I wish I could say the same.'

'Well, if I'm absolutely honest, it's being busy that stops me feeling sorry for myself.'

Graham checked himself. He was about to reply, 'Me too,' but thought it would sound rather trite and self-pitying. He had a well-paid professional job and a company car. Rita was on her feet all day making enough to scrape by.

'You're involved in the Kilbride Muir scheme, aren't you?' Rita observed.

'Yes,' Graham admitted cautiously, wondering whether she was about to turn accusatory.

'I used to walk up there with my dad when I was little. I don't much care for it now – rather bleak for my tastes – but Dad was a great hillwalker. He used to tell me about St Bride who built a church near there. That's what "Kil" means. A sort of cell where she used to pray and spread the good news.'

'How long ago was that?' asked Graham, surprised that the environmental statement for the wind farm had not considered the cultural history of the site.

'Oh, hundreds of years. Way over 1,000 years ago. Actually, I learned later that no one knows whether she really built a church near there or whether she was just a popular saint. Brigid, she was called really, but she usually became Bride in Scotland.'

'Oh, now I've heard of her.' A penny dropped in Graham's memory. 'My mother-in-law is an Irish Catholic and has a Brigid cross on the wall of her lounge. She's a great fan of Brigid. What a surprise. I'd never associated her with Kilbride Muir.'

'Well, I'm a great fan of Brigid, too,' Rita admitted. 'She was quite the match of any of the men of her day. She's credited with many a miracle, which I'm not sure I believe. But she looked after the poor, set up monasteries, founded an art school, worked with St Patrick, converted kings and became a bishop. The Church respected women in those days!' She beamed.

'It sounds like we could do with her now to help us solve these riddles,' Graham quipped.

Rita smiled again. 'What do you think about the Kilfinan Treasure?' she asked. 'Do you think there really is one?'

'Well …' he paused. 'I think, on balance …' he paused again. 'On balance I think there probably is a real treasure. I've tried to ignore the puzzles, but they've lodged themselves in my brain. Whoever's doing it is smart. I haven't set my foot inside a church since a colleague's funeral five years ago, and here I am becoming a God-botherer! Anyway, no time for it tonight,' he grinned, lifting the briefcase a little. 'What do you think?'

'Me, I'm just enjoying them,' Rita replied. 'I miss church, but I have to be down here every Sunday. I enjoyed poetry at school. The rhyming stuff; not the clever stuff that poets do nowadays. It's got me thinking that maybe Mum and I should go along to one of the evening services. A change would be as good as a rest.'

'I'd better let you go. I'm hoping to be away early tomorrow afternoon so you can safely sell all your baked potatoes. Oh, and if anything dawns on me about the poems over the weekend, I'll let you know.'

Chapter Five

3rd May 2017
Bread

Isla Watts pulled into Kilfinan's one remaining filling station after a long day in the office. Mercifully, the garage shop still had milk and a low-calorie chicken and asparagus risotto, which she gleaned from the shelves before joining the queue. While standing in line she succumbed to a chocolate bar and a copy of the local paper on the 'impulse purchase' shelf.

Isla had hoped that this phase of her life would be different. The children had moved south to pursue careers. A year ago she had separated. She had no illusions about what being newly single might mean. She wasn't deluded enough to be think she would be fancy-free and all her problems would evaporate. But she had been confident of forging a new and happier life.

Now, more often than not, she was too tired to think beyond the prospect of an adequate night's sleep and getting ready for work the following day. Money was tighter than anticipated and she found herself under irresistible pressure to work full-time.

A profusion of garden weeds greeted her as she pulled into the driveway. Isla juggled shopping bag, paper and keys and leaned against the door to let herself in. She felt weary. The house looked weary. They both needed a spring clean, preferably a complete makeover, but neither was in immediate prospect.

The risotto waited by the microwave as she poured a large glass of wine and recuperated on the sofa. Leafing robotically through the pages of the *Kilfinan Gazette* invariably induced the same effect – that of reminding her about the banality of small-town tedium. Hunger began to set in and she was on the point of psyching herself up to move through to the kitchen when she spotted an unwittingly ironic item on the church notices page. She chuckled wryly; it might have been her first smile of the day.

> Being human, we require
> Regular food and drink to refuel –
> Each day God is our constant supplier,
> As long ago in that cruel
> Desert, manna fell daily
> Out of the windows of heaven
> For each wandering Israeli!
> Lust not after Pharisees' leaven:
> I, said Jesus, am the one you should heed
> For my bread of life will a multitude feed.
> Eat of this – you'll have Treasure indeed.

The presence of a poem was no surprise to her. Despite it being the first one she'd actually read, she had been aware of clandestine conversations about strange poems in the local paper. Whispered comments often alluded to a 'Treasure' – possibly somewhere near Kilfinan. Seldom did she buy the paper and hitherto she had barely been aware of the existence of church notices. Her purchase had been an afterthought, but once she spotted the poem she felt it had been an intentional and justified expense. As she read the poem a meme somewhere in her head reminded her of an eavesdropped reference to an acrostic.

She looked at the initial letters – 'Bread of Life'. Why was that familiar? It was a term which she'd heard, though was ignorant of its origin.

Rereading it stirred her imagination and she fancied the idea of playing catch-up with the previous entries. But for the moment the microwave beckoned. Perhaps she would function better after sustenance.

Mechanically she consumed her microwave meal, toying with it as slowly as possible to make the scanty portion seem larger than it actually was. The Rioja cancelled out any reduction in calories from the meal but it succeeded in lowering her stress levels before they turned into a headache. Ten minutes later, with a mug of instant coffee she returned to the sofa and newspaper. It was strange that a religious poem should disrupt her normal routine, but there was something intriguing about it, almost like a sudoku or a codeword. Except that in this case she didn't know the point of the puzzle or whether there was actually a solution.

She re-examined the poem. It was obviously religious and preachy, but its lines had a jocular feel as if a prankster was playing a game with receptive readers. She wondered why 'Treasure' had been capitalised. It might help, she thought, to remind herself why Bread of Life had been a vaguely familiar expression. She tapped purposefully on her phone screen and discovered that it was from a Bible verse: John chapter 6 verse 35, apparently. Her knowledge of Scripture had never been more than perfunctory, but was sufficient for her to know that the Bible was divided into chapters and verses.

Isla remembered that a Bible had been tucked away in the hall cupboard. It had been her late grandmother's; a family heirloom to be treated with care. She unearthed it and brushed the cover with her hand.

She returned to the sofa and sat with the Bible in her lap. It was a beautiful piece of work, with its leather binding and gold lettering. She could picture Gran reading it quietly and thoughtfully by the hearth. It hardly showed any deterioration despite the thousands of times it must have been thumbed over the decades. 'Gran must have really cherished and cared for it,' she thought.

The introduction included a selection of key verses arranged by topic, as a help to the reader who sought particular reassurance or guidance. Isla scanned the topic headings – contentment, family, peace … She sighed ruefully. Things that as a teenage girl she imagined life and marriage might bring. Of course, it hadn't been like that. She was sanguine enough to know that it wasn't entirely the fault of other people, a gradual acceptance which had been a long time coming but which now helped her face the future.

She needed to look up the contents list to find John. It bemused her. Would it be the Gospel of John, or John 1, 2 or 3? She tried the first option: the others seemed too short to have six chapters. Eventually, she found the relevant verse – John 6:35:

> And Jesus said unto them, I am the bread of life: he that cometh to me shall never hunger; and he that believeth on me shall never thirst.

'As if,' she thought.

For some reason it seemed strange to see the actual verse sitting there in the middle of the page. Its stark beauty gave her an inexplicable buzz. She wanted to keep reading but the language was too old-fashioned and dense. She was aware there were more modern versions of the Bible and found a website with unexpected ease on her phone. She skimmed the whole of chapter 6 and saw how it was broken into sections – 'Jesus feeds the five thousand', 'Jesus walks on the water', 'Jesus the bread of life', 'Many disciples desert Jesus'. Crazy stuff she half-remembered from her gran.

She started at the top. The account was not the fairy tale she was expecting. The story about feeding the multitude was told in a plain, matter-of-fact way. It seemed like an eyewitness account from someone who was actually there. There was a ring of truth about people wanting to mob Jesus at the end of it, and how he had to retreat to a quiet place. With a sense of anticipation, she read the next section. Just a handful of short sentences about the disciples seeing Jesus walk on the water. Not the overblown, picture-book childhood fantasy she had recalled. The author seemed more concerned with the reaction of the crowd when they realised that Jesus was no longer there.

Isla was surprised by the narrative. It was simple, direct and disconcertingly credible.

She continued reading, hoping to find more 'comfort food' verses about never being hungry or thirsty. But what she encountered was a baffling exchange of peculiar ideas between different groups of men. It ended up with them talking about eating flesh and blood. She wasn't surprised that some disciples were turning their backs on Jesus. If the 'Treasure', whatever it was, relied on her being able to understand all that ancient stuff, she might as well give up now.

And yet, despite the weirdness of the culture, the words of Jesus somehow sounded beautiful and relevant.

Just as she was about to close the website, she spotted something that rang the faintest of bells. Towards the end of the chapter she saw Simon Peter saying, 'Lord, to whom shall we go? You have the words of eternal life.' It was something that she had heard long ago. She stared at it fixedly.

Isla had the strangest feeling. She had started by digging out an old Bible in order to read a sentence which might help to solve a puzzle, and had ended up stepping into a far deeper mystery. She had thought the Bible was a collection of fairy tales that a few old people believed. But it had inexplicably captured her attention in a more compelling and immediate way than a novel.

To her amazement she continued to reread the whole of chapter 6, and then skim chapters 5 and 7. Perhaps there was no actual 'Treasure'. Perhaps the author was just getting you to think about spiritual riches. Isla hadn't particularly enjoyed school and had been glad to leave, but one uniquely inspirational English teacher had introduced her to something called allegorical writing. Stuff like metaphors and similes, which she had first thought were a waste of time, and had then been persuaded were a means of grasping profound truths. Perhaps this 'Treasure' was a metaphor.

She deluded herself that she hadn't got time to waste. That her giddy life was supercharged with action. Her head told her to get on with the evening.

But her heart wanted to explore further. The quest for a 'Treasure' had curiously gripped her imagination.

She put some speculative search terms into her phone on the off-chance they might throw up something interesting. To her surprise, there quickly emerged a burgeoning blog by someone styling themselves as Kilfie. The effect was disconcerting, as if her home town had suddenly become the centre of a hitherto unknown universe. People appeared to be joining in from around the country, asking if Kilfinan was a real place and what it was like to live there. Kilfie's replies were fulsome.

She pored over it with amused disbelief. She could see that three poems had preceded the one she had been so engrossed in. A growing number of followers were offering their views as to what the poems meant. People proffered opinions ranging from hostile to enthusiastic. Everyone agreed that the poems related to Bible verses.

Most people thought they held hidden clues to some sort of treasure though a few felt they were a religious con trick. Some were adamant the poems were a waste of time, others suggested reading around the Bible verses and enquiring into their deeper meanings.

The blog even had a section called 'Agony Uncle' in which the moderator offered confidential support to anyone wanting to discuss faith issues further. At least it gave the blogger's gender away. Whoever Kilfie was, he was clearly devoting a generous amount of time to his replies and offering helpful suggestions.

To her surprise, Isla found herself delving further into John's Gospel in case the adjacent passages shed additional light. While she was reading, despite her innate scepticism, she suddenly became transfixed. In chapter 4 was a story about a woman at a well. It was ever so vaguely familiar. She knew enough about conditions in the Third World to imagine what it must have been like. Blazing heat. A shunned woman with no friends in a culture where all the women would have turned to each other for safety and friendship. A woman so past caring about social convention that she spoke to a strange man, and in a none-too-respectful manner. And then these strange words about water that never ran out. Constant refreshment. If only!

She read and reread it. She could almost hear the mysterious, half-understood conversations first with the woman and then with the disciples. Eventually she looked up at the clock and discovered half an hour had passed without noticing. Reading the Bible for that length of time! Whatever next?

Actually, Isla knew what the next step should be. One of her friends from the Thursday badminton group, Alice, was a Christian. Alice was her favourite doubles partner: hardly an athlete herself, it was enjoyable to pair up with someone who could actually play. Isla texted her to confirm she would be along. A non-committal message. No agenda, no religion. Just a competitive game.

But Thursday morning got off to a bad start. Isla had run out of conditioner, muesli, peppermint tea, bottled water, sweetener and paper hankies, several of which were urgencies. The early-morning queue at the garage shop put her behind schedule and she covered the winding road to Colm's Cross far too quickly. Ten past nine showed up on the dashboard clock just as she pulled into the office car park's last remaining space.

It wasn't a lavish office, more of a portacabin, from which she administered the daily operations of a camping and caravan site. Bookings were going well this year. She looked across at the new pods, the company's pride and joy, which now festooned the home page of their website. She flustered across to her workstation.

'Good afternoon,' came a sarcastic voice from behind her. She hadn't noticed Josh was already engrossed at his desk.

Her forced smile stifled what she was really thinking: 'And a nice day to you too, you little bundle of misery.'

Enthusiasm came hard that morning, but Josh was the first to emerge from grumpy mode. 'Five feedback comments from guests so far this morning,' he suddenly beamed. 'Every one effusive. "Loved the scenery. Fabulous pod. Felt so close to nature."'

'"Friendly staff"?' enquired Isla.

'Yup, that too.'

Isla stared out of the window again. It was as if she'd been blind to the hills and the forest and the loch. 'I suppose they don't get these views where they come from.'

'Too right. One of them's saying they usually sail in a reclaimed gravel pit.'

Isla looked across to the little jetty nestling among the rowan trees. She silently admonished herself for becoming so blasé. And really, she did enjoy her work. And her colleagues, quite a lot of the time.

Despite the steady stream of work, the day dragged interminably. It felt as if five o'clock would never arrive. She could hardly believe she was daydreaming about when she could have a quiet chat about John's Gospel with a friend whom she had previously tolerated provided she didn't do religion.

She was paired with Alice for the final game of the evening which they won by a nail-biting third set after several strenuous rallies. Isla always experienced an endorphin high after playing well. She thrived on the buzz of competition. She felt too positive for religion. The acrostic felt strangely irrelevant but she pressed on regardless, almost out of duty.

'Alice, can I ask you something about the New Testament?' she whispered in a quiet corner of the hall.

Her badminton partner took it in her stride, apparently without seeing anything unusual or embarrassing in the request. 'Fire away,' she replied with a smile.

'Well, it's a bit awkward here. Can I give you a lift home?'

'Offer accepted, thanks.'

They picked up their gear and headed for the car. 'Rob's working late this evening if you'd like to keep me company over a coffee.'

When they reached Alice's house, Isla's brain raced for a casual way of broaching the subject. She would normally have chatted about sport, work and mutual acquaintances, but the prospect of small talk seemed more awkward than simply asking about a Bible verse.

'I suppose you've been following the acrostics in the *Kilfinan Gazette*?' she asked as two mugs and a depressingly healthy-looking plate of cut fruit were laid on the table. Surely they'd burned off enough calories to justify chocolate biscuits?

Alice shrugged and shook her head.

'You must have! You know, the ones on the church notices page.'

'Oh no, we never get the local rag. We're happy at the Baptists'. Why would we look at the church notices?'

Alice received a rapid precis, and reciprocated with a thumbnail explanation of the 'I am' statements. This led into an animated discussion about a potential treasure hunt.

From her shoulder bag, Isla produced some hastily accrued printouts of the poems and selected online comments. As they pored over the evidence, she was struck by various items around the lounge – a Christian CD, a plaque with a verse, a church magazine. They were unselfconscious incidentals among the suburban normality. She noticed the ease with which Alice spoke about her faith, as if it was a natural topic of conversation.

Alice's eyes scanned the evidence, her eyes flicking from verse to poem to blog and back again. She seemed immediately familiar with all the verses, speaking in simple, familiar ways about who the writers were and what they were saying. She mentioned ways in which the poems could be related to the challenges of daily life. But in relation to deciphering the clues to a treasure hunt, she could be of no assistance.

'I can't see any obvious connections or theme,' Alice finally admitted. 'Perhaps I might be starting to spot some patterns, but that's probably just my imagination. Can you leave them with me and I'll call you if I think of anything?' She paused for a while then added, 'I'll tell you what. I love a good puzzle. Shall we be puzzle buddies? Let's have a go at finding this "Treasure" together.'

Isla was momentarily silent. She wanted the prize for herself. 'How selfish I've become,' she mused. She thought about the risk of being drawn into religious territory. Then she surprised herself by agreeing enthusiastically.

'Would you like to join me at our evening service this weekend?' Alice asked with a trustworthy smile. 'It's very lively.'

Isla hesitated as her brain scurried for a polite way of declining.

'I'll sit with you and make sure no one pounces on you,' Alice continued.

'No, thanks, maybe some other time.'

'OK, not to worry,' Alice smiled. 'Do you like cake? Mum forced a wedge into my hand this afternoon and I'm trying to lose weight. Go on. You don't give yourself enough treats.'

When Isla arrived home, she opened the packet containing a generous quarter of lemon drizzle cake. Next to it she found a booklet; it was called *Introduction to Alpha*. She admired Alice's chutzpah. 'Naughty,' she thought, 'but nice.'

Chapter Six

10th May 2017
Mammon

Jim Aubery grudgingly purchased a copy of the *Kilfinan Gazette*. He never usually wasted £1 on its predictable trivia and gossip and only bought it because he was unable to access the website, which had recently crashed. Apparently there had been an uncharacteristically high volume of traffic.

He also begrudged reading the church notices and *Thought for the Week*. He didn't care for religion, but he too had become intrigued by gossip about the prospect of some sort of local treasure.

Not that he needed the 'Treasure', whatever it might be. He was more than comfortably off, even after an expensive divorce. But he liked acquiring stuff, especially costly stuff. And he liked solving problems, especially when he succeeded in producing an elegant solution that demanded respect and envy.

He conceded a grudging admiration for the mystery poet, even though the culprit was probably some religious fanatic. It had not taken him long to reckon on a biblical basis to the puzzles and, with the help of the internet, had tracked down the relevant verses. He had not read beyond them – why should he bother? He felt intuitively that the key to the code lay in the verses, the verse numbers or the poems. He would read the minimum amount of Scripture necessary to break the code.

Jim stuffed the newspaper into his bulging briefcase and retrieved his top-of-the-range Audi from the disabled parking space outside the shop. In all his time in Kilfinan, he had never seen the parking restrictions enforced except on a Monday afternoon when the traffic wardens made their customary visit and the town became a paragon of adherence to street markings. Ten minutes later he pulled into his geometrically paved driveway, grabbed his briefcase off the front seat, and entered the empty house. He scanned the hall and lounge to make sure that Nan, the daily, had achieved her customary level of perfection. Then he poured a large malt and settled on the sofa to read the *Gazette*.

Skimming the paper to confirm that it actually contained no news, he turned to the week's poem. It read:

> No amount of money can buy
> Eternal life:
> Extravagant lifestyles oft belie
> Despair and strife.
> Love of money will amplify
> Evil's root and Satan's lease:
> Steering a camel through the tiniest
> Eye of a needle is simpler than purchasing peace.
> Your most precious coin is rarely the shiniest –
> Endue, therefore, Treasure that will never cease.

Again it was an acrostic and again had a capitalised T for Treasure. '"Needle's eye,"' he muttered out loud. A quick internet search indicated Matthew 19:24, which he printed out. He remembered the expression from school, even recalling the teacher's explanation of how the rich man had to remove his burden of wealth before going through the needle gate at Jerusalem.

Checking out some of the internet references he learned that there was possibly little truth in the teacher's interpretation. He hoped there was no truth, either, in the scripture. Despite his lack of faith, it still managed to prick his conscience. As, indeed, had the previous four poems with which by now he was familiar.

Jim looked around the silent house where he now lived alone. His principal companion was rancour, born of the large amount of maintenance he paid out monthly. Early on, he had succumbed to alcohol to deaden the pain but by now had moderated his consumption and used workaholism as an alternative coping mechanism. Besides, no one could begrudge him his salary if he spent twelve hours a day earning it.

The puzzle was a welcome distraction and it gave him an almost infantile delight, even though he had no idea what the answers meant or how they might be connected. He supposed that any self-respecting treasure would be buried somewhere in the locality and had bought an Ordnance Survey map of the area, having been greeted by the surprising response of 'Not another one!' from the bookseller.

He gave the map greater attention than he had given the *Kilfinan Gazette* in the hope that there might be an obvious geographical feature called the Needle's Eye, or something similar. The smattering of Gaelic he could remember from school still proved handy, especially when it came to understanding local place names. But no obvious places or landmarks drew his attention for this or previous weeks' acrostics. Even so, it struck him as curious that people were evidently buying hard copies of the map rather than, as was now customary, consulting the relevant excerpts digitally. Given the modern reliance on satnav and GPS, it surprised him that people still possessed the necessary skills to interpret a traditional map.

Frustrated, he decided to allow himself half an hour poring over the clues before getting on with what remained of the evening. He looked again at the pertinent page in the newspaper in case it contained hints additional to the poem itself. There was the usual nonsense on offer from the baffling variety of indistinguishable churches. The *Thought for the Week* had some piffle about being neighbourly, which seemed irrelevant to the chase.

He cut out the poem and laid it on the table before him. Around it he assembled other evidence. Printouts of previous weeks' acrostics. Printouts of Bible verses in what he hoped was a suitable translation, selected on the basis of its relative readability among the bewildering choice of online alternatives. Second Chronicles, Isaiah, Matthew (twice), John. An accumulation of scribbled notes. Printouts from Kilfie's blog. Heal the Land, Clay and Potter, Weary Find Rest, Bread of Life, Needle's Eye. It was mumbo-jumbo as far as he was concerned, but he was determined to pit his devious mind against an inferior intellect.

Jim read them over and over, as had become his recent custom. He fancied he was beginning to get a hang of the way the setter thought. It was obviously someone with a Christian worldview, but thankfully not a hellfire and damnation one. It was the work of a person with a spiritual take on life and who probably had a low opinion of material wealth. 'Each to his own,' thought Jim, as he poured himself another malt.

He went back online to check through the blog. Initially, he had wondered whether the mystery poet and Kilfie were one and the same, or at least working in tandem. But the blogger professed to being as baffled as anyone, and appeared to be an honest person in all other respects. Apparently he was unable to offer any firm guidance to solving the clues and ventured few opinions of his own, other than reflections on the spiritual content of the poems and readings. This Kilfie seemed to have started out with little knowledge of social networking but had ascended a steep learning curve on running a personal website, and by now had organised it quite effectively and acquired an impressive number of likes and followers. So, perhaps someone who was on an irritatingly similar wavelength to the poet. An opportunist jumping on a bandwagon to spread his version of the Christian message. In other words, not much use.

Jim considered the possibilities analytically. It was unlikely, he felt, that the acrostics themselves contained further encrypted clues. For one thing, he had examined them closely and failed to uncover any patterns or codes in the letters; for another, he realised it was difficult enough to write an acrostic, especially a rhyming one, and thus improbable that the writer was clever enough to conceal additional levels of encryption. Most likely, it was the work of a local religious bod, not a master code-setter.

He unfolded his map on the carpet. The area was peppered with interesting features and place names. He pored over it for any suggestion, in English or Gaelic, of associations with the acrostics, but failed to find anything convincing, not even a 'traveller's rest'. Many places and features included the name of a saint, but none was Matthew or John. Even an internet search of the wider area had revealed only one church dedicated to Matthew and two to John; hardly a breakthrough.

He returned to Kilfie's blog and began to classify the entries into themes. He enjoyed organising data, sorting out the wheat from the chaff. The first category of posts included those dismissing the treasure hunt as a fool's errand. It was simply a prank by a local Christian with a mischievous streak. A way of getting people to spend a few moments thinking about something spiritual. The 'Treasure' to which the poems referred was nothing more than allegory. Among these posts, the majority view was that the writer had already achieved their aim by getting people to look at the Bible.

The second group of posts were those which presumed there was some kind of spiritual thread in the acrostics. There was something about prayer, searching, listening, fulfilment, reward. Some used the word 'pilgrimage' to describe the leitmotif and related it to the old pilgrim paths and relics of Celtic saints in the area. Many said they had found the poems helpful and had enjoyed rediscovering favourite passages from the Bible. Opinion among these bloggers was evenly divided as to whether the acrostics were pointing to an actual treasure or a metaphorical one. Among the former, there was further debate as to whether the 'Treasure' was buried or whether the solution lay simply in deriving an answer from wordplay.

The third group was from bloggers certain that there was a hidden message which would lead to a specific item of value, but that the acrostic themes were not in themselves significant. There were several attempts to seek word and letter patterns in the poems and Bible passages, but even the most ingenious suggestions proved unconvincing. Some thought the emergent titles of the acrostics held the key; others looked for patterns in the verse numbers. A couple of recent posts suggested the verses might hold a key relating to local place names, and Jim mused whether this might account for the sudden increase in map sales. Unusually, Kilfie had added a personal endorsement to this effect, without giving any useful reason, other than to mention he was long accustomed to navigating the local landscape.

Jim reluctantly admired the mystery poet, who had even succeeded in getting a cynical non-believer like himself to consult chunks of Scripture. He even privately admitted that some bits of the Bible weren't as daft as he'd imagined. Annoyingly, he couldn't get rid of the idea that Matthew 19:24 harboured some sort of personal message for him.

After a while, though, he decided he had spent long enough on a religious goose chase. He arranged the items in a box file, stretched his back and wandered around the lounge.

He didn't feel like doing more work just yet. The treasure hunt had disrupted his evening routine to an exasperating degree. He realised he felt hungry, but couldn't summon up the energy to rummage in the kitchen. He picked up his car keys instead. No matter the whiskies he'd drunk; he had a nonchalant feeling of invulnerability.

He headed off to the Marnock Country House Hotel. The evening was turning to dusk as he drove north from Kilfinan, and he soon became aware he was not alone on the road. Behind him a car maintained a steady distance; the traffic cops often drove in unmarked vehicles around here. He recalled the whiskies. Nanny state! He checked his speed. Fine. And his headlights. Also fine. He was confident he wasn't breaking any law. But the car clung limpet-like at a steady distance.

His stomach began to churn. His inebriated brother had once been stopped for a faulty tail-light, depriving him of his licence for a year and leading to a hefty fine and a brutal insurance premium. He breathed deeply and steadily until reaching the hotel gateposts. As he turned down the gravel driveway, the attendant car drove on, the occupant of the passenger seat staring icily towards the hotel.

Jim took a deep breath, shook his head and regained his composure. He noticed he had been sweating. He was angry and relieved at the same time. The lounge bar beckoned. He considered the restaurant but preferred the bar; dining alone at a table always made him feel self-conscious.

A Polish barman took his order: a large Merlot and a medium-rare steak. Jim didn't care for Eastern Europeans but nowadays the hotels hereabouts seemed to find little alternative. He helped himself to a paper from the magazine rack, pulled over a stool and hunched over the counter. A few feet to his right were a couple chattering eagerly about acrostics. He could scarcely stifle a guffaw. Hopefully they would blab a few clues.

Jim stared up at the wall. He found it more interesting than the fake news in the paper. His mind wandered to the bulging briefcase awaiting him when he returned home. Spreadsheets of weekly sales figures to overlay on market areas and populate with household economic data. In reality, he did not have the slightest need to work until midnight but doing so would put him at an advantage at tomorrow's business breakfast. He could score points off his colleagues. He could outsmart and shred them if he wanted. Who might it be tomorrow? Inwardly, he chuckled with anticipation: he was spoilt for choice. This was how his region would exceed its targets and how he would get his bonus, the size of which was a company secret.

The couple were still discussing acrostics. 'Endue … Treasure that will never cease' he recalled, and smiled. 'Good luck with that sort of treasure,' he thought. 'You're welcome to it.'

Chapter Seven

17th May 2017
Still

Colin White clocked off from the sawmill. It was hard work. It didn't make much use of his school qualifications, but he counted himself lucky to have found a local job, reasonably paid. Many of his mates either faced a long commute to the city or had moved away from the peninsula. On these long summer days, when forestry activity was at a peak, he had little time for recreation. And after the hard physical demands of the day he was happy to hit the sofa. A couple of years ago he would have headed into the hills or visited the local hostelry, but now he was content to unwind with a remote control in one hand and a drink in the other.

A chance conversation a couple of weeks ago had piqued his curiosity about some items in the local paper. He had gone to the King's Arms after work and bumped into an old pal from his Boys' Brigade days. Over a pint, he had learned about some curious poems that were appearing alongside the 'Godslot'. The brigade had been a big part of their lives. Even though their church connections had now lapsed, a religious conversation came more naturally to them than it might to most twenty-something lads.

Colin was quite a fan of the *Gazette*. His previous girlfriend had worked in their advertising office, and it carried articles about people he knew in various local sports teams. Sometimes the forestry business featured, and it had once included a photograph of himself as a newly recruited apprentice, which had been clipped and saved for posterity.

He reached Kilfinan's principal newsagent five minutes before it closed, in search of an Ordnance Survey map of the local area. It had sold out. Picking up the new edition of the *Gazette* he asked the checkout assistant when the map section might be restocked. She shook her head as if to convey bewilderment.

'Another one,' she muttered enigmatically. 'Normally we sell one a week, if that.'

Colin had been following the increased level of activity on social media pertaining to strange verses in the *Gazette*. Among the largely inconclusive speculations and theories about the acrostics, one trend had struck him. For some inadequately explained reason there had been a surge in sales of the local Ordnance Survey map. Most bloggers considered it curious that people would still purchase the 'dead tree' version rather than freely access the same information on their phone. Kilfie himself, though, suggested that the traditional version might hold some additional clues, but offered no specific reason beyond a vague hint that his countryside skills were coming in handy.

On returning to his flat, Colin rummaged in the glory hole beneath the communal stairwell. Somewhere there was a box containing his old Boys' Brigade paraphernalia. It didn't take long to find and, tucked down the side, was what he sought: a collection of dog-eared Ordnance Survey maps. He levered out the one of the Kilfinan peninsula. It was an ageing edition, frayed at the folds and blotched from rain spatters. Still, it was perfectly useable; very little changed around Kilfinan apart from wind farms and forest extensions, so a map continued to serve its basic purpose well beyond its sell-by date. He also pulled out the well-thumbed Bible that he had once used regularly. Of the many activities undertaken in the brigade which had proved useful in adult life, he hadn't anticipated Bible knowledge would be among them – until recently.

He riffled lazily through the box. Its contents produced a frisson of nostalgia for the outdoor lifestyle and camaraderie of his teens. He had loved the walks, the climbs, the secret spots for wild camping. They were now a receding memory, superseded by the demands of work.

He placed the map to one side and settled down on the sofa, can of craft beer in one hand, newspaper in the other. There by the church notices was another acrostic.

> Sometimes we can hear the Lord
> Thunder like an earthquake,
> Impossible to be ignored,
> Lambent as daybreak,
> Luminous and clear.

> Sometimes God's word
> 'Midst flames will appear.
> And yet at times it's heard
> Like the merest whisper.
> Listen intently for that inner, still
> Voice, like silence, yet crisper –
> Often the truest words are the least shrill.
> If you have a special trysting place
> Come to God there, seek His face,
> Encounter His boundless Treasure of grace.

His eyes strafed down the initial letters. 'Still small voice,' he mused. He recalled the expression from a hymn rather than from the Bible, but a quick search on his phone led him to 1 Kings 19:12:

> and after the earthquake a fire, but the LORD was
> not in the fire; and after the fire a still small voice.

To begin with, Colin could not place the story. He felt he should have recollected it easily, but the context had gone. He read the whole chapter, and then chapters 18 and 20 for good measure. Gradually he began to recall the confrontation at Mount Carmel and Elijah's flight from his enemies. In the Boys' Brigade he had once considered himself to be a very zealous person: not in the Elijah league, but actively committed to the Lord. It was stories such as this one about the prophets of Baal that fired and fascinated him. He couldn't recall how or when that passion had drifted away.

Colin was sure that the author of the poems was leading people on some sort of treasure hunt – again the word 'Treasure' was capitalised. He had begun to apply his analytical mind, which his teachers had once praised so much, to the challenge.

'Could it be,' he mused, 'that there is some connection between the geography of the area and the Bible passages, and that is why people are buying the map?'

He knew he wasn't the first to think along those lines. Kilfie's blog had a thread of comments to this effect but it appeared no more than intelligent guesswork, just a promising hunch. One of the comments had also suggested a link to the numerous Celtic saints associated with the area. Apparently, the sentiments conveyed in the acrostics were reminiscent of the supposed qualities of the Celtic Church. This possibility interested Colin. He had read of a resurgence of interest in the early saints. A Christian retreat centre had opened on a nearby island and a walkers' trail had been designated to connect with the already successful St Ninian's Way. He had promised himself to learn more about the local saints and perhaps to tread in some of their footsteps. One of these days, when time permitted.

There was little time for daydreaming at the sawmill, but in his few idle moments Colin did wonder whether inspiration might descend on him if he headed for the great outdoors at the weekend. The latest poem reinforced this idea. He had been struck by its reference to a 'trysting place', a curious turn of phrase he had once encountered in an article on Celtic spirituality. He mused whether serendipity might befall him if he were to study the puzzles in a contemplative spot, far from the distractions of the home and the ease of the sofa.

So he decided against working overtime at the weekend. The weather forecast had been benign and, indeed, Saturday turned out to be a day made for walking, with clear visibility and just enough breeze to refresh weary limbs. He had walked the area extensively since boyhood and, like many folk, had his secret place where he could be alone with his thoughts. This was St Colm's Cave on the other side of the sea loch, a mysterious grotto gouged out of sandstone cliffs above a rocky platform which connected to a rough and usually deserted coastal path. There was rarely another soul to disturb the crashing waves which reverberated around the cave's shadowy interior.

At school he had learned that Colm was the same person as Columba, the Irish saint who settled in Iona and brought Christianity to the northern Picts. Colin had always held a soft spot for Columba. A saint who was learned and intelligent, as well as brave and adventurous, a perfect balance of admirable qualities for the impressionable adolescent. Imagine sailing from Ireland in a wicker currach sealed with nothing more than a skein of leather! An inveterate warrior-missionary who had parleyed with kings. Colin had visited the abbey at Iona a couple of times; its pace of life and its work for justice and peace had left a lasting impression on him. Not enough, though, to encourage him to attend church. In fact, it seemed the polar opposite of organised religion. If he still had a faith, it was a personal, reflective one that didn't need to engage with long sermons and stuffy buildings.

Colin couldn't afford himself a lie-in: he had to make the most of Saturday's limited transport service. He caught the first ferry across to St Kessog's and took the connecting bus to Dunserf, where the seaward path began. After a mile the deserted coastline came into view, the surging power of the Atlantic contrasting starkly with the calm of the sea loch higher up. Visibility was crystal clear and it was one of those rare days when the hills of Antrim could be picked out on the far horizon. It was a long time, far too long, since he had walked over that wave-cut shelf that furnished a path to the cave's mouth. He was fortunate the tide was not high, and he knew from experience that the cave would remain accessible for a couple of hours yet.

Colin stared at the infinite power of the sea pounding the rocks below his feet. He felt a degree of irony. How could anywhere be more different from Elijah's cave – arid and fathomless, an inland haven from the desert heat and vengeful enemies? Yet, even so, St Colm's Cave seemed to share that same atmospheric tranquillity and potential for spiritual encounter.

After a while he produced from his backpack a chocolate bar, water bottle, Bible and bedraggled map. He felt intuitively that the last of these must contain a pointer to the 'Treasure'.

He opened the Bible and read First Kings chapter 19 again. As he stared at it in the dappled half-light he fancied he could hear a still, small voice. It must have been his imagination. He waited intently for inspiration. Nothing.

But he was in no hurry. It was an effort to get here and he didn't want to leave any time soon. He could spend another hour listening to the sea, staring into its depths and watching the cormorants flying and diving in defiance of the waves. Currently in between girlfriends and with many of his friends seeking pastures new, he was accustomed to his own company.

As he gazed at the glistening lichen-encrusted rocks, he again imagined he heard a voice. It was probably autosuggestion, he reasoned, yet it seemed to tell him quite specifically to reacquaint himself with the Elijah story. He couldn't resist the faint but insistent prompt in his head. Slowly, reflectively, he browsed chapters 16 through to 22. It was an episode he had once studied closely, but now only recalled the haziest details about folk such as Ahab, Elisha, Naboth and Jezebel.

As he perused it, he realised why it had held such a fascination for his adolescent self. It was a remarkable narrative, as gripping as any adventure novel. Even if it didn't help him discover the 'Treasure', he felt his time had been well spent. He felt none the wiser about the acrostics and assumed that he must have imagined the still, small voice. Although one aspect did strike him. He noticed how precise the author of First Kings had been. Why had so much attention been paid to numerical details? Doubtless these would be significant in ancient culture. There were two caves, fifty prophets in each, 450 prophets of Baal, 400 prophets of Asherah, twelve stones, four jars of water, forty days and nights, 7,000 faithful, twelve yoke of oxen. Numbers, numbers – the idea that these might be important lodged itself in his mind.

He stared at the map again to see if he could spot any connections. There were no place names bearing any obvious resemblance to the themes of the poems. And what, if any, significance might numbers have? Spot heights, road numbers? He scanned the map from side to side, up and down, trying to detect anything that might be more apparent on a hard copy than on a smartphone screen. It was like staring into a fog, unable to see a signpost that should be in plain view. Patently, copies had been selling unusually well, so it was quite possible that some people had spotted a clue. There again, it might just be a meme. Or perhaps some people were expecting the 'Treasure' to be buried somewhere in the local countryside.

Then he noticed something very obvious, something so familiar that it hadn't even registered. Numbers round the edge. Grid references. He wondered if he could still remember how to take a reading. In the Boys' Brigade, calculating the northings and eastings had been second nature. He checked the map legend for the worked example, then worked out the reference for the grid square in which he currently sat. Noting the two-letter prefix, he then calculated the numerical part. The eastings read 19. He measured the northings – 12. A light bulb lit in his head. Hadn't the Bible verse been 19:12?

A flock of black guillemots floated impassively in front of him, oblivious to the surging tide. He would normally have gazed in wonder at them, but now was not the moment for contemplation. He picked up his items and tripped along the slippery rock ledge as quickly as safety would permit. He jogged along the steep and stony path and was relieved to find an expectant queue at the bus stop. Public transport was sparse at the weekend.

Back at his flat, he could find no time for lunch. A chocolate bar and glass of water sufficed.

He spread a collection of notes about the acrostics on the table. If 1912 had led to St Colm's Cave, might there be similar clues in the other verses?

The first poem had referred to Second Chronicles 7:14. This made no sense as a four-digit reference. After lengthy reflection he wondered whether it would be worth checking 0714. This grid reference led him to a square containing Kilbride Muir. He had learned at school that Kilbride meant the cell church of St Brigid. It might be a long shot, but he dared to wonder whether there might be an association with local saints.

He went with trepidation to the next reference – Isaiah 64:8, or 6408 as he reckoned it would be. But it lay too far to the east. A quick rummage in his box of tricks unearthed the adjacent map, in even more dog-eared condition. His briefly raised hopes were dashed. The square was in the middle of an expansive moor, with no named features. The middle of nowhere, crossed by an isolated path. Sheep country.

No, he must be mistaken. But a still, small voice told him not to be discouraged.

The next reference had been Matthew 11:28. Grid square 1128 took him to an ancient monument, a ruin known as St Blane's Priory. His heart began to race again. He had a strong sense of being on the cusp of solving the puzzle.

Perhaps the following poem would add confirmation. The reference had been John 6:35. Square 0635 was right at the top of the map and, squeezed in at the edge, he found St Fillan's Chapel.

He went with unbounded optimism to the square suggested by Matthew 19:24. But 1924 took him to open sea. Nothing, just water, water everywhere. Colin wanted to feel downcast, but the surge of excitement still compensated for any temporary disappointment.

Perversely, he retained a buzz of discovery and felt in his soul that this was only a temporary impasse.

And beyond that, the still, small voice had implanted itself. The more he thought about it, the more he was sure it had been there and had not deceived him. He remembered that once upon a time he used regularly to listen for a still, small voice. As an adult he had lost contact with prayer and daily readings, without ever consciously losing faith.

His experience in the cave had reminded him how much he had drifted from his spiritual roots. How much he had come to prioritise self and rely on his own abilities; how beholden he had become to the clamour of the world's competing voices. It had afforded him time to reflect on his direction in life, if nothing else.

But he felt certain there was indeed something else.

Chapter Eight

12th March 2017
Inspiration

Penny Waite drew the morning communion service to a close with the benediction as Sam watched from the wings. Priesthood suited her better than either had expected, notwithstanding their high expectations in the first place. In all the time they had been married, Sam had never seen her so much at ease with herself. How she had agonised over the decision, about giving up the success and status that went with a business career. Yet once she had been ordained, there had never been a moment's regret. She was in her element: a natural shepherd of a gradually growing flock.

Sam experienced a shard of envy. He had successfully balanced life as a full-time engineer with lay readership and had imagined that early retirement would afford him opportunity to develop a distinctive ministry while continuing to accept the occasional piece of consultancy. Yet retirement had brought as much frustration as fulfilment. The freelance business opportunities had never materialised, although this was not something he overly regretted. He had found his occupational pension covered their living costs adequately and such were the horror stories he now heard from former colleagues about the modern workplace that he was happy to maintain a discreet distance. His lay ministry had its rewards, yet it only partially satisfied his aspirations for the future. More often than not, he felt like a bellhop covering for gaps in the deanery rota. Useful but ineffectual; it was as if the old Sam 'Makeweight' was re-emerging.

Sam's life wasn't an unenviable one; indeed, perhaps it was too comfortable. He had no regrets about bidding farewell to the day job and was held in affection by the St Finnan's congregation. He enjoyed the invitations to preach elsewhere in the diocese.

Yet when he first moved to Kilfinan he had felt called to do so much more. He wasn't an evangelical firebrand and he sidestepped numerous entreaties to engage more actively in mission and outreach. In his heart, what he most wanted was for people to discover and return to a deep personal faith. Sam was concerned with quality rather than quantity. He enjoyed sharing his experiences with people on spiritual journeys of their own, whether churchgoers or not.

He especially desired that people would blow the dust off their Bibles – if not for spiritual enlightenment, then at least for its wisdom and poetry. Sam loved the Scriptures. He wasn't a Holy Joe and he didn't find every word of the Bible easy or straightforward. But he was saddened by its marginalisation in Western culture, even among many churchgoers. In many parts of the world people were desperate to get hold of Bibles; here, too often, they gathered dust on forgotten shelves.

But he reckoned that any idea of getting people to read the Scriptures again was a pipe dream. Many local ministers had launched initiatives to encourage some form of Bible study or personal devotion, to little avail. So, without a focus in life, Sam bumbled on from day to day.

After several months of retirement, Penny grew irritated by his apathy and apparent unwillingness to talk about whatever was troubling him. She put it down to an inability to adjust after nearly four decades of intensive professional work.

'Sam!' she exclaimed in exasperation one day. 'You need a project. Not more meetings and committees, but something that will get your oomph back.'

'Have I become dull?' Sam asked, insipidly.

Penny didn't want to upset him, but the words 'as ditchwater' were past her lips before she could check herself. Sam looked crestfallen. Penny forced an encouraging smile and put her arm round his shoulder.

'A year ago you were full of ideas and energy. Now you're just going through the motions.'

She hoped Sam could tell she had said it out of love, not anger. He was quiet for a minute, apparently wondering how best to respond.

'Well,' he said eventually. 'There's something I've been mulling over. It's daft, really. It wouldn't work.'

'No defeatism allowed in this rectory,' Penny retorted. 'Sit down and tell!'

'One thing that really saddens me is how little people know the Bible. Even people who go to church. I suspect that many of them hear a short reading on a Sunday morning and that does them for the rest of the week. In many parts of the world people are literally risking their lives to get hold of a copy. I wish I could at least plant a little seed that would start to change that.'

Penny nodded in agreement. Sam sounded genuinely cross, as if he actually did possess well-hidden depths of passion. Her immediate instinct was to introduce a campaign at St Finnan's to get the congregation to follow a set pattern of daily reflections. But before the idea had formed into a sentence, she realised it would be yet another 'initiative'. She reined in her impulse to speak before engaging her brain. 'No, it's not that simple. Let's think it through,' she thought.

She surprised herself at the length of her silence. Penny's long silences generally did not augur well and she knew Sam would be preparing for the worst. But when her answer eventually came it was sanguine and sensitive.

'Sam, that's a very noble idea, but it would be terribly difficult to achieve. I've challenged people to develop a deeper understanding of Scripture; I've left devotional notes in the church, and some of them have even been taken, but I've no idea whether they've been read. Lots of ministers have tried, but I don't know of any who've had real success. What makes you think you'd succeed where they failed?'

'No, you're probably right. It was just a fancy. I'd had a barmy idea that if I linked it to some sort of puzzle and treasure hunt people might get more motivated.'

Penny straightened. Her features tautened with anticipation. 'Now you're talking. Had you anything specific in mind?'

'I know this sounds really daft, but… well… the gospel is like a pearl of "great value". Isn't that what it says in Matthew 13? What if I hid a pearl somewhere and left clues that required people to search for answers in the Bible?'

Penny beamed. Yes, it really was a crackpot idea. But it was no dafter than many of the other proposals that had been mooted. And, above all, it was Sam's idea. Anything to get him out of his rut. At length she suggested, 'Do you remember when you gave me that card on my ordination? You put an acrostic verse in it. Could you do something like that?'

Sam looked blank for a moment before emitting a bashful chuckle. 'Oh goodness. I'd almost forgotten. It's not like me to be spontaneous and creative, is it? I recall it took me ages.'

Penny bounced up from her chair. 'I'll dig it out. It's in my bedside drawer.'

'You don't mean to say you kept it?' Sam's voice was tinged with pleasant surprise.

She returned after a minute. 'There you go!'

Sam looked at his first and only attempt to write a greeting card verse:

> Realise now your most heartfelt vision –
> Every one of us has a lifelong dream;
> Very few of us make such a brave decision
>
> Putting aside pride and self-esteem.
> Each day now you'll have chances to enthuse,

New lives to transform, new hearts to inspire,
Never doubt your ability, and never lose
Your passion, your vision, your faith, your fire.

When he had first penned it, Penny could tell that Sam had been quite impressed with himself. She had considered it gauche but had refrained from saying so because its sentiment was quite touching. Seeing it again, Penny thought it had a certain merit, while Sam's face betrayed embarrassment at its amateurishness.

He blushed: 'Rev Penny! Oh, I'm sure I could improve on that!'

Penny didn't demur; for the first time in weeks there was fire in his eyes. She had an unusually positive sense that Sam was on the brink of a workable idea. At the very least it would provide him with some harmless amusement. At best, he might actually achieve his ambition to get people to rediscover their Bibles. She watched as he gambolled through the French windows into the garden. The bulbs were just starting to bear shoots. There were buds on the shrubs. It was a good time of year to be creative. She knew that after a good night's sleep on the matter he would start in earnest.

Next morning, a ground frost glistened as the fragile northern sun made its hesitant appearance. Sam could tell it would be a day that required a pullover rather than a waterproof. He checked the 'his and hers' calendar in the rectory kitchen to confirm that today his half was indeed totally blank. It was a perfect occasion on which to select a well-known Bible verse and see if he could manage to write a rhyming acrostic about it. After breakfast, he retreated to his study with a purposeful air. But the more he tried to put pen to paper the more he struck the buffers of writer's block.

A little over an hour later he looked at his initial effort and cringed. He crumpled the paper in embarrassed dismay. The task was proving far harder than imagined. Anyway, he began to realise that picking random verses wouldn't actually lead people to a hidden treasure. He was starting on a journey which as yet had no departure point, route or destination. It was an unusual experience for Sam, whose cardinal if ponderous virtue was that of conceiving and executing projects down to the last minutiae.

The matter needed much more thought. How would the treasure hunt work in practice? Would there be an actual treasure? Would it need to be hidden somewhere so that the explorer had to dig it up? If so, might the treasure be damaged or accidentally discovered? Was it possible for the puzzle to just lead to a paper solution that would enable the winner to make contact and claim their prize? How would he bring the acrostics to people's attention? Would the puzzle be soluble? Would anyone actually bother with it?

By the end of the week, Sam was becoming despondent. He was on the point of abandonment, and Penny had to break off preparing an impending sermon to offer emergency support. Together they sat down to investigate a workable solution and, after numerous blind alleys, an ill-formed possibility began to emerge. It commenced when Penny randomly observed: 'There's a lot of interest in Celtic Christianity at the moment. Some folk from our church went on a retreat recently where they looked at the lives of early saints. Apparently it attracted several people who were just on the fringes of faith and didn't have a church connection. It's just a thought, but there are a lot of saints referred to in place names around here. I wonder if you could somehow incorporate them into a puzzle?'

Sam's imagination stirred. He knew the notion of Celtic Christianity was something of a chimera but he was very much attracted to the early, simple roots of the Church. There was an immediacy and generosity in the faith of local saints which had somehow succeeded in spreading the gospel in a hostile environment. It was definitely the best idea so far.

'They're well represented in this area,' Sam remarked. 'In fact, seven of them are represented in our vestry window. That's a hidden gem. Very few people are aware of it.'

Sam could see that Penny's brain was about to go into overdrive, but he checked her.

'You've got a sermon to prepare,' he reminded her. 'Now, thank you for the idea. Let me mull it over and leave you in peace.'

He put on his walking boots and tugged his rucksack from under the stairs. 'See you in a few hours,' he called as the door shut behind him.

Sam's best thinking was done in the hills, particularly on their local 'Munro', Beinn Bhreac. The sensible way to climb it was to drive to the Forestry Commission car park a couple of miles from town where a well-beaten track led to the summit. However, there was also a lesser-used route which could be reached on foot from the rectory. Sam chose the latter as it enabled him to concentrate on the figments in his head rather than on the traffic.

A mile after he had ventured off the road down the moorland path, he was struggling to locate his position on the map. The profile of the hill looked very different from this angle and a sphagnum bog confronted him. The correct way must be somewhere nearby, but it was far from obvious. He studied the contours, the position of the sun. He rotated the map and angled it against the path and the burn. Eventually he figured the route and identified a faint line where the passage of boots had worn away some of the vegetation.

As he continued along the mountain's initial slopes, he was suddenly struck by a possibility for linking places to Bible verses. It was a long shot and possibly too technical but, in his view, not wholly impractical. He abandoned the walk and loped back to the rectory.

Penny was still working in the study and greeted him with an affectionate wave without lifting her head. It was best to leave her in peace. Sam crossed over to the church and entered the vestry. It had a small window, barely more than a lancet, which bore skilful stained-glass miniatures of saints with local connections. It wasn't well known, even among the St Finnan's congregation, who were far more aware of the fine panel depicting their patron saint in the west transept. The window was mentioned in a couple of local imprints as well as a website of historically and architecturally significant ecclesiastical buildings, so it shouldn't be impossible for the determined sleuth to track down.

The challenge would be to link specific verses to local geographical features which bore these particular saints' names. The scheme that had occurred to him on Beinn

Bhreac seemed technically feasible. Further, he felt it shouldn't be too difficult to find appropriately named locations – there were any number of settlements, old buildings, archaeological relics and landscape features named after saints in the vicinity. He was determined to give it his best shot.

Over dinner he explained his idea to Penny. It was unusual for Sam to do all the talking, except when he was detailing the mechanics of a tortuously conceived project. Indeed, perhaps he was subconsciously giving her little opportunity to speak because he suspected her reaction would be unfavourable. She wore the detached expression that she reserved for his more technical and geekish proposals: yet, in the end she tilted her eyebrows in a way that conferred acquiescence. Sam had clearance to take it to the next level.

Sam took a coffee to his study and started working. He readily identified various local place names referring to the six saints who comprised the figurative border of the window: indeed, he discovered there were so many direct and indirect references to saints in the locality that the degree of choice would make the selection of appropriate Bible verses relatively easy. He had less success with the seventh saint which sat in the centre but eventually realised that its omission could work to his advantage. After barely an hour of trial and error he succeeded in choosing distinctive verses that corresponded to his code.

During the next week, Sam succeeded in producing acrostics that pointed reasonably unequivocally to the Bible verses he had chosen. The methodical, ageing 'Makeweight' was suddenly like a child with a new toy.

When he finally showed the verses to Penny, her face was one of unfeigned approval. He was surprised at her enthusiastic endorsement that this might just succeed.

It was only when he was on the point of finalising his plans that Sam suddenly got cold feet. He realised it could be an expensive task. The prize would be a pearl, and not a cheap one. Moreover, the only way he could think of bringing the acrostics to the public's attention was to purchase space in the local newspaper. And what if it didn't work? What if the only people to take an interest were those who were already regularly reading their Bible and attending church? What if it was just ignored? Or it was too easy? Or too difficult? Or won by someone who didn't care two hoots for the Bible?

Penny was out on a pastoral visit, a particularly sensitive and difficult one. Sam desperately needed to talk to her because he trusted her judgement. He was on the point of ditching the idea altogether. When Penny eventually returned she looked emotionally drained and Sam hadn't the heart to add to her woes. So he kept his thoughts until the morning, by which time he had convinced himself that the idea lacked the slightest merit. It was ill-conceived, convoluted, costly and destined to fail. He should turn his attention to more pressing and productive tasks.

Over breakfast, they finally had time to discuss the matter. Penny harboured misgivings but didn't want to say so immediately. She hadn't yet had her 'quiet time' and her head wasn't in the right place. They agreed to mull it over and Sam departed into the garden to manicure his beloved shrubbery, while Penny sauntered across to the vestry where she kept her diocesan study notes. This morning they were on Matthew 13. She smiled. How appropriate for a man tending his garden!

After half an hour, Penny joined him, beaming. 'Sam,' she announced in her buoyant, non-negotiable voice, 'you've got to do it. Honestly, it will work. If it's too difficult, you can publish additional clues, but I have a sneaking suspicion someone will hit on the solution.'

Sam was astounded. It was unlike Penny to display such irrational excitement. He waited for an explanation.

'Sow the seed, Sam. Just sow the seed.'

However much he trusted Penny's judgement, Sam needed something more than a whim. His mouth opened to ask for enlightenment but before a word could emerge Penny added: 'When you post your last puzzle, I'll make sure it's my turn to write *Thought for the Week*. Then you'll understand.' She winked.

A wink from Penny was more reassuring than a cogent argument from anyone else. Whatever the explanation, he knew she would be right.

Chapter Nine

26th May 2017
Serendipity

Despite the main tourist season not yet having begun, the 'No Vacancies' sign once more hung outside *Mon Abri* guest house. The single room vacated by Graham Coe for the weekend had a new occupant. Katie Smith had an uncanny sense of why he was here. He looked neither like a local worker nor a stereotypical outdoorsy holidaymaker; his well-maintained face had an air of urbanity and intellect and his clothes were slightly too formal. He smiled aloofly as he sniffed around the compact room, but he was not impolite.

'I hope the room's suitable. Would you like me to make you a cup of tea?' Katie enquired.

Tom Hodson nodded winsomely. 'Yes and yes,' he replied. 'I've had a long drive from the Midlands and detoured for longer than advisable on the other side of the loch. Almost missed my ferry.'

Katie was impressed with his perfectly executed 'ch' rather than saying 'lock'. 'Oh dear, that would have been a pity. It would have meant a long wait or a tiresome drive round the top of the peninsula. The ferry service isn't as good as it used to be. Were you distracted by the scenery?'

'Actually, there was somewhere up in the moors I needed to visit en route. I took a leg-stretch along a section of St Ninian's Way. Only for a mile or so, just to get some fresh air in my lungs. Have you heard of it?'

Katie tried to stifle an expression of curiosity. 'Oh yes,' she replied, simply. 'I gather it's becoming quite popular.'

Tom settled in the parlour and chatted inconsequentially over tea, cakes and an unsolicited round of sandwiches before returning to his room. Katie could see he wanted to settle down to some unspecified business for he was evidently pleased at the sight of a small desk by the bedroom window. As she closed the door, Katie saw him riffle a collection of papers and sundries from the incongruously smart leather briefcase.

Tom had not taken a weekend away by himself since his engagement. A widower, he had recently found late love with a widow of similar age. If Ruth had been aware of his unaccustomed departure for the west coast of Scotland – and the reason for it – she would have been highly amused. Tom found it curious that a scientist like Ruth should be a person of faith. She would have found it equally comic that a non-believer like Tom should be delving into a Bible and unmasking saints.

He had stumbled across an internet discussion about an apparent treasure hunt centred on the town of Kilfinan, a place of which he had never heard but which was in an area he had harboured a desire to visit. He had soon discovered several Facebook pages chronicling the shared thoughts of treasure seekers as well as a dedicated blog. He even took out a subscription to the online edition of the local newspaper.

His fiercely rational brain had quickly spotted elements that proved more elusive to others: that the poems were acrostics; that they consistently related to a 'Treasure'; that they alluded to specific Bible verses, and that the chapter-and-verse numbers looked suspiciously like fairly adjacent grid coordinates. He had identified the relevant verses with only minimal recourse to the internet. Despite his lack of faith, Tom retained a decent knowledge of Scripture from his schooldays.

From there, it was a short step to experimenting with grid references on the local Ordnance Survey map. This immediately bore fruit and, when the 'needle' puzzle led him to open sea, his Bible memory was still sufficiently accurate to remind him that the same story appeared in two Gospels. He checked the alternative reference in Mark, which yielded 10:25, in turn leading him to a square containing an antiquity called St Marnock's Well. His newly acquired maps were, fortunately, the latest editions and the eastern moors showed the recently designated long-distance path, St Ninian's Way, the name of which occurred in 6408.

Up to this point the Kilfinan acrostics had been a source of amusement rather than an active quest. However, the latest issue of the *Gazette* contained a poem which clearly seemed to signal an end point:

> Perhaps you have followed our quest,
> Each of six saints you have guessed
> And yet there's a seventh to put into the mix

Ringed within the other six –
Locate it, and with Treasure be blessed.

The timing was fortuitous. Ruth was away visiting her sister so he was a free agent; if a suitable bed and breakfast had a vacancy he could inspect the locality at first hand and make a concerted attempt to solve the riddle. On checking Kilfie's blog, he redoubled his determination. The blogger was in equally little doubt that this marked the end of the clues. And for the first time Kilfie betrayed something of his own position, writing: 'I think I may now have the solution, but feel that I have a professional advantage, and so will leave it for another to find.'

If Kilfie was hot on the trail, so might others be. There was no time to lose.

He devised a route that would take him via part of St Ninian's Way, of which he had printed out an interpretative leaflet from a pilgrim trail website. He hadn't been surprised to learn that few hard facts existed about Ninian. The saint was credited with starting his mission to Scotland in AD397 and so reliable details were understandably lost in the mists of time. However, an education in Rome seemed likely and he might have met St Martin of Tours, before establishing a centre in Whithorn. Ninian was probably buried there and, in the ensuing centuries, his shrine became a destination for pilgrims.

'Good for him,' thought Tom. Despite his lack of faith, Tom was a big fan of pilgrimage. It was a companionable tradition, he felt, and one which merited its current revival. He fancied that he and Ruth should walk St Ninian's Way at some stage. Apart from anything else, Whithorn was on his shopping list of visitable places, and to arrive there on foot seemed entirely fitting.

After hours on motorways it had made a pleasant change for Tom to be heading into the remoter countryside and finally to reach the single-track road that led across the moor. Grid square 6408 lay a short distance from the lane, but the weather was fine and Tom didn't resent the walk. He surveyed the area but, as expected, did not see anything unusual or distinctive about the stretch of path. It reinforced his view that the reference was simply to the saint's name, not to an on-site object or physical pointer.

He wished he could linger but realised he was still some way from the guest house and could ill afford to erode his precious time in Kilfinan.

On finally arriving at his destination he encountered the legendary hospitality in this part of the world. The portions of food which accompanied Katie's pot of tea were so ample that he had no need to seek a meal that evening. Realising that the northern daylight would last at least another couple of hours, he stuck to his plan to visit the remaining sites before nightfall. Again, he doubted if actually seeing them would cast light on the solution, but he felt they might give him inspiration. Before setting out he checked the bedside table and was not surprised to find a Gideons' Bible. He read through the pertinent verses one more time, just in case they contained hints that became more apparent now he was breathing Kilfinan air.

Tom's tour of the area proved enjoyable but unilluminating. Hills, forests, moor and sea lochs were not his natural environment. He was a creature of the lowlands and preferred rolling agricultural pastures interspersed with quaint villages and country pubs all within striking distance of metropolitan culture. But he could understand the appeal of the wild, the possibility of escaping the thrum of traffic, the unpolluted air. He visited Kilbride Muir, dotted with sheep and sprouting a small cluster of wind turbines. With powerful binoculars he gazed across to the wild coastline where St Colm's Cave was tucked away. He visited the supposed site of St Marnock's Well where a swollen burn tumbled beneath a stone bridge, and then continued to the nearby ruin of St Blane's Priory, neatly tended and marked with an informative plaque. To his surprise, he found St Fillan's Chapel still in use and unlocked; he felt a degree of humility at being in a corner of the world where doors didn't need to be secured. Inside, he gazed at the ancient saints depicted in its windows and felt a genuine admiration for their courage in bringing the gospel to a hostile audience in an untamed land.

He returned to *Anam Cara* that night with an enjoyable feeling of having peered into the time-depth of the area, and a growing belief that he was closing in on a solution. There had been no physical clues awaiting him at any of the sites: indeed, he would have been surprised if there had been. His next recourse would be to visit the local library in the hope that its history section might reveal the significance of saints Brigid, Ninian, Blane, Fillan, Marnock and Colm. A good night's sleep and the eagerly awaited 'full Scottish breakfast' would fortify him for the task.

Kilfinan residents valued their local library and had fought a rearguard action with the council to keep it open on Saturday. Indeed, as he waited outside the door at 10.00am, Tom was pleasantly surprised to see that it did not shut until 4.00 in the afternoon. The place was evidently less philistine than his own town. The duty librarian gave him a knowing look as he asked for the local history section and pointed out the books most likely to be of interest. She mentioned that some older texts had recently been retrieved from storage in response to a sudden upsurge in interest.

He started with a general local history of the area written by a retired headmaster in the 1970s, venerating the great and the good of the locality, of which there had been a surprising number. It was clearly a place deserving more than a passing degree of respect. However, the monograph contained little about the area's earlier history or older Christian heritage, or indeed its geography or archaeology. He made a few notes and turned to the next book in his pile. As he looked up from his desk he noticed other eyes casting judgemental glances at the selfish mound of texts he monopolised. He smiled and returned the first book to the shelf, from where it was quickly retrieved by a poorly complexioned youth.

His next two books, little more than pamphlets, were old but creditably scholarly accounts of locally important families and church history. These gave him occasional insights of potential value, especially one which alluded to early saints. Nowadays, an author would have embellished the narrative with some fashionable jargon about Celtic Christianity, but this prose was restrained and erudite. Even so, and despite the questionable accounts of some of their exploits, one could not help but admire their saintly qualities. Marnock, the missionary bishop of the seventh century who had been under the tutelage of

Columba. Brigid founding her abbey. Fillan blessing a well that helped to treat the demon-possessed. Blane's erudition and piety. Ninian's and Colm's brave adventures upon the sea. The narratives were informative and even inspirational, but offered little additional enlightenment relative to the task in hand. Tom's internet research had already been thorough.

Reluctantly he returned books to the shelves after extracting as much information from them as possible, all the time keeping a sharp eye for some annotation or illustration that might hint at a key to the puzzle. Each time he returned a book to the shelf, other eager hands retrieved it. He fancied their enquiries would be equally in vain.

By lunchtime he had exhausted the books suggested to him by the librarian and resorted to the nearest café to mull over his next step. It was beginning to seem that he would return home the following day empty-handed: no richer, but better informed and slightly humbler. He felt that such an outcome was probably justified. Far better that someone local, even a person of faith, should find the 'Treasure', if such a thing existed.

He scanned the poem in the paper one more time in case it contained some cunning final indication. He had still not satisfactorily fathomed why the initial letters should spell 'pearl'. By itself, it did not lead to a specific Bible verse, and he wondered whether he was missing a key. He cast a sceptical eye across the church notices, each of which offered their particular, and purportedly unique, path to salvation. There was even an advert for a Bahá'í gathering and he supposed that opposition to its teachings would be the one thing that would unify the various Christian denominations. He muttered in bafflement.

The only other content on the page was the *Thought for the Week*, this time from the local Episcopal priest, Penny Waite. He recognised the verse on which it was based – Matthew 13:23: 'But the seed falling on good soil refers to someone who hears the word and understands it. This is the one who produces a crop, yielding a hundred, sixty or thirty times what was sown.' The parable of the sower was one he recalled well from his schooldays. He doubted whether it pointed to eternal life but he thought it a shrewd story, and one which helped to convince him that Jesus was an actual historical character. The four types of personality described were instantly recognisable from daily life. The oblivious one, the fair-weather adherent, the one whose mind was always on something else, and the one who listens, comprehends and acts.

He looked at what the priest had to say about the story. He felt it wasn't half bad – practical and not too preachy. The writer spoke about the declining appreciation of the Bible in our society and how believers and non-believers alike could draw benefit from its wisdom. She pressed home the point about understanding and perceiving rather than merely hearing and seeing. Tom was impressed that a woman of the cloth should encourage her readers to question things more deeply. 'Risky,' Tom thought. 'They could end up like me.'

And as he read the piece he had the faintest sense that it connected with the acrostics. Could the writer know more than she was letting on? Could he be the one who was not perceiving and hearing – along with all the other treasure seekers? He dismissed this thought as fanciful and scanned the page one last time before folding his paper away.

At two o'clock he returned to the library to avail himself one final time of its facilities. He surveyed the shelves: crime, sci-fi, romantic fiction… He ruled out the likelihood of the answer lying in such categories and browsed the modest non-fiction and reference sections instead. Tucked away in the reference section were some pamphlets of local information which he had not yet noticed. Information about businesses, public transport, council services and other topics of local significance. One was a booklet produced by the 'Churches Together' group with interesting detail about the various congregations and ministers. He read it thoroughly for any hints but learned only about the fellowship and sincerity of the parishioners who had written the entries for their particular churches. He was really quite touched.

The final pamphlet was more intact than might have been expected for a short print run by a local publisher: *Account of Some Historic and Architectural Points of Interest in Kilfinan.* He felt a frisson of promise; he certainly hoped so because his options were running out. Indeed, he was tending to the view that there was no real end point after all, just some crafty Christian getting people to read the Bible and discover spiritual 'Treasure'.

At the back of his mind he recalled something about treasures in heaven, which aren't corrupted by moths or stolen by thieves. He felt a degree of grudging admiration.

He opened the booklet. It was more detailed and better illustrated than he had anticipated. He read about finials on the village hall, mock-Mackintosh houses alongside the glen, fishermen's cottages by the wharf and sepulchres in the Catholic church graveyard. And then he spotted something of extreme interest. The entry on St Finnan's Episcopal Church observed that it was a pretty building from the late nineteenth century with a few notable features, one of which was a small window in the vestry containing stained-glass illustrations of seven locally significant saints. Unfortunately it did not say which ones, but the fact that there were seven was enough to send a shiver down Tom's spine. Clues to six saints, and a hint at a mysterious seventh. Perhaps the solution lay in finding the missing name? If so, it would be a tremendous stroke of serendipity. Of course, had she known, Ruth would have insisted that there was no such thing as coincidence.

The Episcopal church sounded familiar. Then he remembered the *Thought for the Week*. 'Aha! Perhaps Penny Waite does know something we don't,' he mused. He felt a sensation which he had only rarely experienced in his adult life – that of barely being able to contain his glee.

Tom tried his hardest to maintain a poker face. He steadied his hand as he replaced the book on the shelf, pushing it unfairly far back so that it was hardly visible. He mimicked a sigh of resignation as he perfunctorily browsed some other shelves before strolling out of the library, giving a polite smile to the staff as he exited.

He returned to *Anam Cara* to freshen up and change into something a little smarter, before embarking on one final piece of research. He indulged in a moment of mild satisfaction and anticipation, tinged with a twinge of guilt at the insincerity of his Bible study. He dispelled this compunction with an admission that it had not all been in vain. He had genuinely been pleasantly surprised by his encounter with the Scriptures and places of worship. Whether he was on the cusp of a discovery or whether he was on a wild goose chase, he resolved to pass by St Finnan's the following morning on his way home to watch the faithful arrive for Eucharist. If their clergy were as savvy as he suspected, they and their flock deserved at the very least an admiring gaze.

St Finnan's did indeed prove to be a pretty little church. Outside was a noticeboard bearing the incumbent's name: Penelope Waite, BA BD. Next to it was a poster showing a merchant gazing at a pearl in his hand, and a verse which read '"upon finding one pearl of great value, he went and sold all that he had and bought it" Matthew 13:46, NASB'. A satisfied smile suffused Tom Hodson's face.

Postscript

Penny perused the front-page article in the *Kilfinan Gazette*, in which Sam finally revealed his identity and purpose. It was abundantly evident that the venture had been well received. The reporter remarked on the exceptional level of interest generated by the Kilfinan Treasure, but withheld the details of its discoverer, noting only he was not from the peninsula.

The following day, she picked up the mail which had dropped through the rectory letter box. The first item was addressed to them both. Penny looked in puzzlement at its solitary, anonymous content. She examined the smudged postmark; it might have said Nantwich, but she could not be sure. She beckoned to Sam to take a look. Smiles of realisation simultaneously dawned across their faces as they read the missive:

> Kilfinan's mystery has been solved –
> It led ordinary folk to discover a
> Lamp to their feet, a light to their path,
> For Scripture is God-breathed,
> Is useful for teaching and training,
> Equipping us for every good work,
> Is more precious than gold,
> Sweeter than the honeycomb,
> And it brings great reward.

Rediscovering their Bibles, people
Checked chapter and verse,
Hoping therein to find clues
Illuminating the way to treasure.
Each in their turn discovered pearls,
Gleaned something special
In unexpected ways.
Let us now leave Kilfinan
'Midst the forest, hill and moor
Over the sea, across the shore
Under the peaks where eagles soar,
Richer with blessings than before.

If you've enjoyed meeting Penny and Sam, you can learn more about their distinctive ministry in their adoptive home of Kilfinan in Harry Hunter's earlier book, *Taking the High Road*.